TENSE

VOLUME ONE

NEW YORK TIMES BESTSELLING AUTHOR
DEBORAH BLADON

FIRST ORIGINAL EDITION, APRIL 2017

Copyright © 2017 by Deborah Bladon

All rights reserved. No parts of this book may be reproduced in any form or by any means without written consent from the author.

This is a work of fiction. Names, characters, places and incidents either are the product of the author's imagination or are used factiously. Any resemblance to actual person's, living or dead, events, or locales are entirely coincidental.

ISBN-13: 978-1545301463
ISBN-10: 1545301468
eBook ISBN: 978-1-926440-43-9

Book & cover design by Wolf & Eagle Media

www.deborahbladon.com

Also by Deborah Bladon

THE OBSESSED SERIES
THE EXPOSED SERIES
THE PULSE SERIES
THE VAIN SERIES
THE RUIN SERIES
IMPULSE
SOLO
THE GONE SERIES
FUSE
THE TRACE SERIES
CHANCE
THE EMBER SERIES
THE RISE SERIES
HAZE
SHIVER
TORN
THE HEAT SERIES
RISK
MELT

Chapter 1

Sophia

"Do you like it? Some people have said it's too long. It's thick when you're holding it in your hands, isn't it?" The tone is masculine. It's low and throaty, emanating somewhere from my right.

Such is the conversation on subway trains in New York City. You'd think I'd be oblivious to it all by now. Most people who have lived here for decades have an innate ability to silence the staccato sounds of voices, traffic, and the underlying hum that is constantly hanging in the air in Manhattan.

For those of us who are considered recent transplants, the timbres of the city are still a part of its undeniable charm. I never thought I'd grow accustomed to the constant buzz beyond my bedroom window when I closed my eyes to sleep each night, but now it's the lull the helps me drift off. I've only been here for two years, but I know I'd crave the frenzied energy of this place if I ever decided to move back home to rural Florida.

"I'd like your honest opinion." I feel the slight pressure of a shoulder rub against mine. "Chapter seven is my personal favorite. Have you gotten that far into it yet?"

I glance down at the thick book resting on my lap. I now know, without a doubt, that he's talking to me. I've already had two, one-sided, conversations about the book today. The first was with a woman waiting in line at the dry cleaners. The other was just fifteen minutes ago with the man who owns the bodega by my office. In both cases, I just smiled, nodded and listened to them rattle on about the awe-inspiring detective novel I'm lugging around Manhattan with me.

"I haven't," I answer without looking at him.

No eye contact will make it easier for me to ignore him if he persists. I'm not a rude person, but I do know how to protect myself with a perimeter of ignorance. Men give up quickly if you pretend they don't exist. Most men do, that is. This one doesn't seem to be taking the hint.

"What page are you on?" A large hand brushes against my navy blue skirt. "You've made it past the first chapter, right?"

Physical touching is a no-no. I scoot more to my left, trying to gain a few more inches from him. This train is bursting at capacity with commuters. Part of that is the time of day, and the other is the route.

It's early evening, and I'm Times Square bound. It's one of the few places in the city I'd be happy never seeing again. It's not for me. There are too many people, too much noise; the smells are overwhelming, and the pace is frenetic.

"I'm not trying to accost you." He laughs. It's a sexy growl and a few women turn to see the source. Judging by the way they linger when they look at him, he's not hard on the eyes.

"I'm just trying to get to a book signing," I confess, hoping he'll leave me alone if I tell him, politely, that I'm not looking to hook up. "I need to get this signed for my boss. It's a birthday gift from his wife."

"You're hoping to meet the author? Nicholas Wolf? I heard the line for the signing is around the block. People have been waiting since this afternoon to meet him."

"Dammit." I finally turn to look at him. "You're not serious, are you?"

He's as good looking as I imagined him to be based on his voice. Seriously hot. As in, I-will-give-this-man-my-number-if-he-asks-for-it, hot.

Black hair, blue eyes and the stubble shading his jaw are the appetizers. A perfect smile, chiseled features and his lips, oh those lips, are the main course. He's wearing a dark wool coat and jeans so who knows what dessert is, but it would be delicious. I know it would be delicious.

"I'm serious," he says. "If you get in line now, the store is going to close before you get that book signed for your boss."

I roll my eyes. "I don't get the appeal. I have no idea why Gabriel likes it so much. He told me to read it, so I started to read the first chapter and…" I point my thumb toward the floor.

"Thumbs down?" He knits his brow. "You didn't like it?"

"It's too wordy. I was so bored I couldn't finish it."

He stares at the book before he speaks again. "I take it Gabriel is your boss? You're getting it signed for him?"

I nod sharply.

"Give it to me. I'd like to show you something."

It's not my book, and since we're moving at breakneck speed inside a subway car, it's not as though he can grab it and run. I slide it from my lap to his.

"What's your name?" he asks as his hand dives into a brown leather messenger bag slung over his shoulder.

I watch his every movement. "Sophia. My name is Sophia. What's your name?"

He pulls a silver pen from the bag and before I can protest, he opens the cover of the book and starts writing.

Well, shit. I bet it's his number. I'm not going to stop him. I'll just buy another book for Mr. Foster and keep this one for myself.

He closes the cover of the book with a firm snap, slides the pen back into the bag and turns to look at me. "My name is Nicholas. Nicholas Wolf."

"Sure," I scoff. Does he think I was born yesterday? The author of the book that he's holding in his hands is way too successful to be riding the subway to his own book signing. Nicholas Wolf must have a driver at his permanent disposal to take him wherever he wants to go. Besides, all I need to do is pull out my phone and do a quick search for the renowned author. Judging by the verbose text in the book, Nicholas Wolf is a ninety-year-old retired English professor. "You think I'm naïve enough to fall for that? Nice try but you're not him."

"You don't strike me as naïve." He flips the book over and raises it so the back cover is next to his face. "See the resemblance?"

I've never bothered to glance at anything other than the moody artwork on the front cover and the few scant pages I forced myself to read. There, in the corner of the back cover of the book I've had in my possession all day, is a small headshot of the man sitting next to me.

There's a smug grin on the face of the guy I'm talking to. The photographic version on the book has a sexy scowl, shorter hair and a pair of black rimmed glasses framing his gorgeous eyes. I doubt I would have recognized him as the same person even if I was aware of what the illustrious Nicholas Wolf looked like before I sat down next to him.

Dammit. I insulted him. I told him his book was boring. It's the same work that's won him numerous awards and landed him a spot at the top of every bestseller list there is.

"I should probably apologize for what I said about your book." I try to force a smile.

He narrows his eyes as he studies me. "Were you being honest when you said it was boring?"

I've got nothing to lose at this point. There's no way in hell he'd believe me if I told him I was teasing him about his book being a snoozefest. I didn't like it. I'll never see him again, so there's no reason for me to be anything but truthful.
"I wasn't lying," I confess, but I don't stop there. I need to buffer my words because I know what it feels like to have your creative work torn apart. There are enough bitchy comments on the pictures I've posted

to social media to last me a lifetime. Not everyone likes the clothing I design and I'm the first to admit that it stings to read anything negative about something I've worked tirelessly on. "I should mention that I've never read a detective novel in my life. It's not my thing so please don't take my criticism personally."

"What's your thing?"

I squint at him, trying to decipher what's behind the question. He's still grinning, a clear sign that he didn't take my insult about his work to heart. His skin must be thicker than mine if he can face criticism without even a minor flinch. "What do you mean? What thing? Are you asking me what type of books I like to read?"

"I'm not asking that, but let's start there."

I swallow. "I don't want to start there. I want to know what you meant."

The noticeable slowing of the train draws the commuters around us to their feet. "You'll have to wait until tomorrow at lunch to find out. I have a book signing to get to."

"Tomorrow at lunch?" My eyes follow his movement as he stands. "I'd remember if we had a discussion about lunch tomorrow."

"We didn't. I wrote the details down for you in the book."

I flip open the cover to see an address in the West Village and the words *'tomorrow at noon, Sophia'* scribbled in blue ink. He didn't sign the book so I could give it to Gabriel. He used it to invite me to lunch.

"This isn't my book." I sigh. "I can't give this to Gabriel's wife now."

"I have an advance copy of my next release in here." He pats the front of his bag. "I'm reading a chapter tonight before I answer questions and sign books. It's yours if you'll have lunch with me."

Why do I feel like this total stranger is coercing me into sharing a meal with him? He's hot and normally I'd find an interaction like this charming, but he still has that arrogant grin plastered on his face. He's confident I'll show and what's worse is that he knows a big part of that isn't related to the book in his bag. "What if I can't leave the office at noon tomorrow?"

He takes a half-step closer to me as people start to migrate to the door so they can rush off once we stop. "Tell your boss...tell Gabriel who you're meeting. He'll probably give you the entire afternoon off and maybe even a bump in pay."

I'm all for self-confidence but Nicholas Wolf's ego is in a league of its own. I want that book though. Mr. Foster isn't just my employer, he's finally becoming a friend and I'd give almost anything to see the expression on his face and on his wife, Isla's, if I present them with a yet-to-be released book written by their favorite author.

"I'll see you tomorrow, Sophia." His fingertips graze my shoulders. "This was a pleasure."

A pleasure? That's one way to describe it. I'm leaning more toward the word *clusterfuck* but maybe that's just me.

Mr. Foster's birthday is tomorrow and I have nothing to show for it, other than a lunch invitation from a man who clearly sees himself as something special. He might be, hell, he obviously is, but men like Nicholas Wolf are a dime a dozen in Manhattan. They know what they have to offer and they're all too aware that their charm is almost irresistible.

Almost. I know that I can resist.

All I have to do is show up for lunch, get my hands on that book and take it back to the office before the sun sets on Gabriel's birthday.

It's as simple as that.

Chapter 2

Sophia

"Are you the same Sophia Reese who texted me an hour ago to say she was going to a book signing?" My best friend, Cadence Sutton, thinks she's funny. I can tell by the huge smile on her face.

"I decided to skip it. I thought you could use the company since Tyler is at work." I peer past her into the living room of the apartment she shares with her fiancé. "I brought you some ice cream from that place you like. I was going to stop at the deli to get a kosher pickle, but I know you have a nine month supply in your refrigerator."

She rubs her small belly. "I'm trying to cut back on the pickles this week, Soph. Tyler's worried that the sodium content is too much for the baby. My new, healthier, craving is banana chips."

"My brother cracked a tooth on one of those when we were kids. You might need to steer the craving train onto another track. What about regular bananas?"

She steps aside to let me in before she closes the door behind me. "I had a banana craving right after I found out I was pregnant. Tyler called me Monkey for two weeks straight."

"That's not some awkward segue into your sex life again, is it? If it is, I'm bowing out now and heading back to my place."

Technically, my place belongs to Cadence. I moved in with her shortly after I landed in New York from Florida. Since she's taken up residence with the love of her life, I've had two different roommate-from-hell experiences. I'm living alone now but hopefully, I can find someone to fill the empty bedroom soon. Cadence never complains about the fact that I pay next to nothing for rent each month. She's told me I can live alone as long as I want, but it's too large of a place for just one person. Besides, I'm always looking for someone I can use as a human mannequin to model my latest creations for me.

"You're not going anywhere." She runs her hand through her shoulder length blonde hair. "Come inside and tell me why you ditched the book signing. Did you realize on your way there that you don't read books?"

"The line for the signing was too long and for your information, I read books," I protest through a smile. "I'm always reading."

"Fashion magazines don't count."

I step into the living room and look beyond the wall of glass at the lights that dot the evening skyline. "I wasn't talking about Vogue or Glamour. I meant that book on the history of fashion. I read it from cover-to-cover last summer. Twice."

"Now that you mention it, I do remember you burying your nose in that book." She reaches for the pint of strawberry ice cream in my hands. "When my baby is our age, people will be writing not only articles about your designs, Soph; they'll be writing entire books about you."

Grateful, I dart up to my tiptoes to softly kiss her cheek. Even though I'm wearing three-inch heels, my best friend still has a few inches on me. It doesn't help that I stopped growing mid-teens when I reached the five foot two-inch mark. "You make me feel like I can accomplish anything, Den."

"You need to start believing more in your talent, Soph. Your designs are going to take the world by storm as soon as you catch the eye of someone with influence. I keep telling you to show Mr. Foster the lookbook on your website. You know if you did that, he'd move you over to the creative department on the spot."

I don't know that. Mr. Foster has a vision for all three divisions that fall under the Foster fashion umbrella. I haven't tried my hand at designing anything for men or any lingerie, so if I'm going to make a pitch to him, it would be for the women's line. I've kept a constant eye on everything they've released since I started working as his assistant.

The line, and the boutiques the clothing is sold at is named Arilia and although my stuff would fit, it's not an ideal match. My ultimate dream is to have my own collection, but for now, if I could get a few pieces accepted into Arilia boutiques, I'd have a solid base to build on.

"When I decide on which designs to pitch him, I'll do it," I say honestly as I shrug off my vintage white wool coat before I fold it over the back of a chair. "The way I see it is I get one chance to impress the man. I know what he likes so once I create something that he can't say *no* to, I'll be in his office with a sample to show him."

"I could choose at least twenty pieces right now. Why don't we meet at your place for lunch tomorrow instead of here? We'll skip the wedding planning and pick out some of your designs so you can show your boss that his assistant is the next big name in fashion. I'll make your favorite sandwich and that raspberry lemonade you love."

A smile tugs at my lips. When Cadence asked me to be her maid of honor, I cried. Tomorrow is our first official wedding planning session. I'm supposed to meet her here at noon sharp so she can cook me something decadent for lunch while we discuss the venue, the guest list and flowers. One of the perks of having a professional chef for a best friend is delicious lunch meetings.

I silently follow her into the kitchen and watch as she scoops the pale pink ice cream into two white ceramic bowls. "Which one do you want?"

I laugh as I reach for the half-filled bowl. "You can have the overflowing one, Den. You're eating for you and the little mister. I'll take this one."

"You're a gem." She slides a spoon of the frozen treat into her mouth. "This is so good. No one in this city makes ice cream like Cremza."

I take her word for it because I try to avoid anything too sweet. I gingerly eat a spoonful before I break the news to her. "I can't do lunch tomorrow. I met a guy on the train tonight. He asked me to meet him at a place in the West Village at noon."

She stops just as another spoon of ice cream nears her lips. "You met a guy? As in, a guy you're going on a date with tomorrow?"

"Lunch isn't a date. It's a casual meeting."

That's where my dating barometer has been set for years. If a guy asks me out for coffee or lunch that's a sign of mild interest. If his first invitation is for dinner I know he's into me. There was one guy who asked if I wanted to go home with him while I was waiting in line to renew my driver's license at the DMV back in Florida. I didn't take him up on his offer but judging by the erection that was straining against his thin sweat pants, his interest in me was off the charts. At least it was until I told him I wasn't looking for a random hook-up and he started flirting with the woman behind him in line.

"What's his name?" Cadence runs her index finger over the corner of her mouth to catch a dribble of melting ice cream.

As tempted as I am to tell her every detail of my exchange on the subway with Nicholas Wolf, I don't. Den would recognize his name immediately. A copy of one of his books has been sitting on the coffee table in her living room for the past few months. It was a birthday gift from her mom. She hasn't read the book yet. The only time it's moved is when the table is dusted.

If I confess that he's the man I'm meeting, she'll make it into a bigger deal than it is. I know that from experience.

A picture of me talking to the very available star pitcher of the New York Yankees went viral six months ago. A gossip blog picked it up from a photographer who happened to be trailing him. There was nothing between us other than a brief exchange on a corner in Midtown when he asked me if I knew where a certain two-star hotel was. I pointed him in the right direction and then he kissed my hand in a token of gratitude before he darted across the street. I turned to watch him go and the photographer zeroed in on my face.

That brief encounter made my picture the trending topic on social media for an entire twelve hours. I wore the hashtag of #halesbabe for less than a day until someone from work recognized me and tagged me in one of the posts. I tweeted that I didn't know Trey Hale and that I'd never been to a baseball game.

Cadence thought it was fate, so she bought two tickets to a game and a Hale jersey for me. I fought her on it but we ended up at the ballpark bored out of our minds.

Any mention of Nicholas Wolf's name now and I'll stir up the matchmaker in her again. I don't need that. I'm more than capable of finding a man to date on my own when I'm ready. Preferably it'll be one who doesn't have a fan club.

"I asked what his name is." She picks up my bowl of ice cream and finishes the last scoop. "The guy you're meeting for lunch. Tell me his name."

"Nick," I say clearly. "It's Nicholas."

"Nick," she repeats back. "I like it. Where did you meet him?"

"On the subway."

"That's either romantic or creepy."

"It's neither. I sat next to him, we talked and tomorrow we'll meet him for a quick lunch."

"You don't seem excited." She narrows her eyes. "What's wrong with him?"

His ego is the size of Long Island and he blackmailed me into meeting him. Other than that he's perfect.

"I don't know him so I can't say what's wrong with him." I manage to plaster a fake grin on my face. "Ask me again tomorrow afternoon and I'll tell you."

Chapter 3

Nicholas

    If I pride myself on anything, it's my ability to focus. Give me a chair and my laptop, and I can churn out a chapter or two in the middle of Grand Central Station on a Saturday afternoon. My brothers call me the King of Compartmentalization.
    It serves me well. I get my job done and I keep my publisher happy. I haven't missed my self-directed, daily word count in over a year.
    The last time I fell off pace I was nursing a massive hangover brought on by the equally impressive advance check I'd cashed the afternoon before. I drank myself into a fog and ended up in the bed of a woman who didn't have an ounce to drink.
    The frequent text messages she sent me for weeks following that night didn't impact my writing at all. It did serve as a reminder that I'm apt to say just about anything if I've had too many beers.
    I told a stranger I loved her and wanted to marry her. She took it to heart, yet I couldn't remember a thing. For that reason, and that reason alone, I limit myself to one drink at a time.
    Yet, today, I'm on my second scotch and it's just past one o'clock in the afternoon.
    I blame Sophia, the petite brunette with the beautiful blue eyes I met on the subway.
    I didn't bother to get her surname or her number last night before I took off for the book

signing. I thought I wouldn't need it. I assumed she'd be at this restaurant at least fifteen minutes before I showed up at noon sharp.

Women tend to be punctual when you've got something they want. That might be a reservation at the trendiest bistro in the city. It could be the chance to spend a few hours with one of the most successful novelists in the world. More often than not it's the unspoken promise of what will follow the meal.

I don't ask women to meet me here because I want to spend an afternoon describing my creative process. I meet them here because it's less than a block from the apartment I occasionally use as an office. I write there and when the mood strikes, I fuck there.

I follow the same routine each and every time.

It begins with lunch at my regular table in the corner of this bistro at noon sharp.

If my date is receptive, we take a walk to my office.

By early evening I'm on my own again with the physical ache gone and my mind sharp and clear.

I want more. Hell, I need more, but it's not that easy.

My face is on the back of six worldwide bestsellers. Shirtless pictures of me taken in a gym locker room have been morphed into too many memes to count.

Women send me nude photos of themselves. I get propositioned on a daily basis.

Ignoring it is an option but why the fuck would I do that? I revel in it.

I'm riding this crazy train until I decide it's time to step back into reality. From where I'm standing now, I've barely left the station.

"You're Nicholas Wolf. Sophia didn't tell me I'd be meeting you."

I look up and into the face of a man with dark hair. He looks like he stepped out of a boardroom. I, on the other hand, look confused as hell. "Who are you?"

"Gabriel Foster." He extends a hand over the table. "Sophia, my assistant, sent me here."

"She told me about you." I shake his hand, but I don't offer the seat across from me because there's no need. He's settled into it, his palms on the top of the table. A thick gold wedding band circles his ring finger. "And your wife."

"Isla." The way he says her name tells me he loves her. I feel an unexpected sense of relief. It shouldn't matter to me whether Sophia is fucking her boss, but for some reason, it does. This guy is too starry-eyed over his better half to touch another woman.

"Beautiful name," I offer with a raise of my glass. "Will Sophia be joining us?"

I already know the answer to that. I half-expected her to race to catch up with me when I exited the subway last night. I slowed from my regular pace to a leisurely walk with the hope that she'd fall into step beside me. She hadn't. After that, I spent the next two hours scanning the faces of the legions of women packed into the bookstore in Times Square waiting for me to autograph books, arms and yes, even the top of one's tit. Sophia never showed.

He shakes his head. "She gave me a birthday card an hour ago with this address. She told me I'd be meeting someone special here. I've got to say, I assumed my wife would be sitting here waiting for me."

"Sorry to disappoint." I chuckle. "I was under the impression I was meeting Sophia for lunch."

"Really? How well do you know her?"

I know she stood me up. She sent her boss to collect the promised book on her behalf. "Not well. We're barely acquaintances."

"So you assumed Sophia was meeting you and I showed up? Is that what this is?"

He's as polished as every high powered executive I've ever met. I know his type. Everything has a place in his world, including his assistant. If she fucked up and put him in the middle of an embarrassing situation, her ass is on the line. I highly doubt he views her as irreplaceable.

"Sophia arranged for me to give you a gift." I reach into my bag and pull out the book I promised her last night. "Your wife asked Sophia to get me to sign *Burden's Proof* for you, but Sophia requested an advance copy of my next release."

"*Action's Cause*?"

I nod. I take great satisfaction in his knowledge of my work. He may run an empire that's successful enough to afford him the Rolex he's wearing, but he's practically salivating at the sight of the book in my hands. "I'll sign it to you."

"To my wife." His finger darts in the air. "I realize it's meant to be a birthday gift for me, but Isla is by far, the biggest fan you have. Sign it to her. I. S. L. A."

I suppose what they say is true. Sacrifice comes in many forms when another owns your heart and soul.

I sign it quickly, my signature an illegible curl of dark colored ink.

After sliding the book across the table, I finish the last swallow of scotch in my glass. "I'd buy you a drink to toast your birthday but I've got a deadline to meet."

It's bullshit. My current deadline is more than a month away and I'm on track to meet it later this week. Sharing another second of my time with this guy isn't part of my day's plan; seeking out Sophia is.

"Understood." He stands. The book I just signed is clutched firmly in his hands. "I'll keep this under wraps. I know you don't want details leaked before release."

"I appreciate that." I do. The book is set to hit shelves and e-readers in less than two months and review copies have already gone out. Spoilers are an inevitable part of the process but keeping them to a minimum is advantageous to not only me but more importantly, to my publisher.

The hastily pulled together reading and signing last night was the brainchild of my publicist. She's determined to create such a high level of buzz for *Action's Cause* that sales will surpass everyone's expectations. She's proven that she can work magic, so I follow her lead.

"I can't thank you enough for this, Nicholas."

"It's my pleasure." I open my wallet and toss a few bills on the table before I push to my feet. "Sophia is the one you should be thanking. This was all her doing."

She's the one who managed to get the book into his hands without having to step foot near me. It's impressive. It's also annoying as fuck.

"I'll thank her as soon as I'm back at the office."

"Tell her I said hello." I pat him on the shoulder as I brush past him on my way to the exit. "And, if you wouldn't mind, tell her I'll be in touch."

Chapter 4

Sophia

He'll be in touch? What the hell does that mean?

"He said he'll be in touch with me?" I question Gabriel. "You're sure Nicholas used those words?"

"I realize it's not my place to ask, Sophia, but is there something personal going on between you two?"

My eyes drop to the book that's open on the desk in front of him. He summoned me to his office when he returned from lunch. I didn't know what to expect when I gave him that card with the address Nicholas had written down when I was sitting next to him on the subway. All I knew was that I wanted Gabriel to have that book, but I didn't want to be the one to get it for him, so I copied the address into the generic birthday card I bought on my way to work, drew a happy face on the envelope and gave it to my boss at noon. I wasn't even sure Nicholas would still be waiting for me by the time Gabriel got to the bistro.

Last night after I got home I did what any single woman should do before she goes to meet a virtual stranger for lunch. I did an online search. Typing Nicholas Wolf's name into Google yielded tens of thousands of results. The top result was his website, the rest of the listings on the first page were reviews of his books.

It wasn't until I clicked on the image search that I uncovered a treasure trove of information. It seems that Nicholas Wolf has one standard sorry approach that he uses to pick up women. It's not only weak, but it borders on narcissism in its worst form.

The second I saw a picture of a woman holding a book in her hands with an address in the West Village written in it, I knew I'd never step foot in the place. When I spotted a second image with a different woman holding a book with the same address, I cursed aloud.

The guy I met on the subway last night uses his own books to pick up women. He writes down the address of that bistro in a copy of his book, meets for lunch and then probably takes them to the hotel around the corner for a quickie.

I suppose the book is a parting gift of sorts.

Thanks for the fuck. Here's a copy of the book I wrote so you can remember our mid-day roll in the hay.

That might not be exactly what he says to the women he has sex with, but it has to be close.

"Nothing is going on between the two of us." I shake my head vigorously. "I met him on the subway when I was on my way to his book signing, sir."

"You must have made quite the impression on him." He smiles. "You coerced him into giving me a book that hasn't been released yet. I don't know how you did it, but I'm forever grateful."

I tricked him. No special skills required.

"I told him you enjoyed his work and he offered the book." Under the pretense that I'd show up at the place he met both of those women who posted pictures of his invitation on their dating blogs.

I don't have a dating blog. You have to actively date to have one of those. What I do have is a book that technically belongs to Mr. Foster in my desk drawer. I wonder if he'd notice if I ripped out the page with the restaurant's address written on it and the personal invitation Nicholas offered to me.

I somehow managed to get out of this without my boss being aware that I sent him on a mission to get his own birthday present. I don't want to press my luck by showing him the book that Nicholas used as date bait to try to lure me in. I need to pick up a new copy of *Burden's Proof* on my way home and give that to Mr. Foster tomorrow.

I'll burn the other copy. I got what I wanted. That means I never have to see Nicholas Wolf or speak to him again.

***

"Is that you, Sophia?" A now familiar voice asks as the man, that I stood up at lunch, approaches from my left. "What are you doing in here?"

I saw him enter the bookstore a few minutes after I did. I might not have noticed him if it wasn't for the loud gasp that came from the female store clerk when he walked past the check-out desk. Apparently, she knows exactly who Nicholas Wolf is.

"I'm buying one of Andrew Star's novels," I drawl as I adjust the books in my hand. "I've heard it's one of the best detective mysteries ever written."

"The only person who would have told you that is Andrew Star."

I roll my eyes. "I doubt that he's the only one who enjoys his work."

"His mother might but I met her at one of my signings last year so it's doubtful."

"As much as I'd like to stand here and listen to you talk about how great you are all night, I have some place I need to be." I take a step to the right, my ponytail swaying with the movement.

He moves to block my path. "You had to be some place this afternoon and you blew that off. You can blow off whatever your plans are now to talk to me."

"I didn't blow you off." My cheeks flush, not just from the burst of anger I feel but from the double meaning of the words. "I sent Gabriel to get his gift because I knew it would mean a lot to him to meet you."

A smile teases his mouth at my small admission. "So you admit that I have some talent? Gabriel strikes me as an educated, cultured man. If he likes my work it must have some merit, agreed?"

"There's a guy in Times Square who wears boxers and paints his entire body silver every day. Then he acts like a robot for tips. Gabriel took a selfie with him one day. Perceived talent is all in the eye of the beholder."

"You're comparing my work to a guy who parades around in his underwear?"

"I guess I am." I nod. "I don't like his work either but plenty of people are fans, including my boss."

"Are you actually going to read Star's book?" He dips his chin toward my hands. "I can summarize it for you on the spot and save you the money."

I'm not planning on reading either of the two books I'm currently holding. I only picked up Andrew Star's book when I spotted Nicholas heading my way. Right now, it's covering the copy of *Burden's Proof* that I came in here to buy.

"This is a spoiler free zone." I circle my elbow in the air. "I want to savor every page of Mr. Star's masterpiece."

"I thought detective novels weren't your thing." He rubs his jaw. "If I remember correctly your exact words were that you've never read a detective novel in your life."

"There's no time like the present to start." I nudge past him, my shoulder rubbing against the heavy gray sweater he's wearing. "I might as well do it with the best."

"The best?" He grabs my arm, his breath whispering over my cheek. "If you want to start with the best, Sophia, open the copy of *Burden's Proof* that you've been trying to hide since I walked in."

Shit.

Double shit.

I turn quickly so I'm facing him directly. I look up into his face. Christ, the man is handsome. He's also ripped under those clothes. I saw a few pictures of him shirtless last night.

There was one meme about uncovering the mystery beneath his gym shorts. My eyes drop to the front of his jeans before I level my gaze on his mouth.

"The book isn't for me. It's for Mr. Foster. You ruined the copy his wife gave to me so I need to replace it."

"Ruined? How?"

"You wrote that address in it."

"I wouldn't call that ruined."

"I don't want him to know that you were expecting to meet me at the restaurant. He would be pissed if he knew I set that up without either of you knowing what was going on. It would humiliate him and he's not the kind of man you humiliate."

"You could have come with him." His gaze pins me in place. "Why didn't you?"

My fingers flex over the books. I should be honest and tell him that I didn't want to fall prey to his charms like countless other women probably have. I could have gone to that restaurant and followed him wherever he wanted to go.

I'm due for an earth shattering orgasm but I'd hate myself after it was over. I'd feel used and regret it. The only person who can protect my self-esteem is me and a man like Nicholas can smash it apart by taking me to bed and then pushing me out the door.

I don't need a marriage proposal after sex, but I need a conversation or two. Experience has taught me that. It's also taught me to trust my instinct about whether a man seems the post fuck discussion type. I'd be surprised if Nicholas takes the time to engage in anything other than a quick goodbye once he's had his fill of a woman.

I don't want to feel used by a man ever again.

"All I wanted today was that book. Once I decided to send Gabriel to meet you I didn't see a point in tagging along."

"You only wanted the book?" His gaze narrows.

"Yes," I admit. "That's all I wanted."

He straightens. "I'll have my publicist send a new copy of *Burden's Proof* to your office tomorrow. Don't bother with Star's book, Sophia. It's shit."

"I can buy your book." I fish in my purse for my wallet. "I don't expect any favors."

"Consider it a thank you gift."

I stop moving. "For what?"

"For being brutally honest with me about my work."

"Honesty is the best policy, right? If you knew anything about my work, I'd expect you to be honest with me. It's the right thing to do." It's also the rude thing but I'm past that. I insulted his work and I can't say I regret it.

His mouth twitches. "Do you want my honest opinion on your work?"

I force back a laugh but a smile escapes me. "You can't critique something you know nothing about. The only thing you know about me is the fact that I don't like your book."

"Is that so?"

"Yes, that's so." I widen my stance.

"I know that you're too talented of a designer to be sitting behind a desk answering phones all day. You're an assistant at Foster Enterprises when you should be the head of their design department."

"Who told you that?" I ask trying to hide the sudden surprise I feel.

"Your work speaks for itself." He opens the browser on his phone and types in my website address.

My eyes flutter over the screen and the images of my two most recent designs. They're maternity dresses, made specifically for Cadence. She's the model although no one would know that. I've always cropped out her face because I don't want her brand to become tangled with mine. My best friend is not only engaged to one of the most talented chefs in all of Manhattan, but she's also a rising culinary star in her own right. She's the host of a weekly food segment on a national morning show. If the world knew that she was the one and only model on my website, it would create a conflict of interest for her.

One of the contractual requirements of her job is that she has to wear an outfit from Bluenix when she's on air. It's a new boutique on Fifth Avenue that's as aggressive with their marketing as they are with their designs. Most of the outfits Cadence has worn have been created by Evlin Dawn. She left Arilia two years ago to launch her own line and she's never looked back. She's only one year older than I am but she's living my dream.

"Why are you an executive assistant?" Nicholas raises his chin and looks down his nose at me. "I'm not a fashion expert but everything on here is stellar. You're wasting your talent."

"It's not that simple." I frown in frustration. "It takes work to be a designer. It can take years to hone your craft. That's what I'm doing now."

"You're hiding behind a poorly designed website. What are you afraid of, Sophia?"

My blood boils, as much for the anger I'm feeling as the embarrassment. He's right. He's hit the nail directly on the head. I'm scared. I'm terrified that my designs will fail. I'm petrified that no one, other than Cadence, will see any value in them.

"I'm not afraid of anything," I lie. "I told you that you know nothing about me. This proves it."

He tugs both books from my hand. "All this proves is that you're an awful liar. You need to learn how to take a leap of faith."

"I know how to do that." I gaze down at the books. "Writing fiction is nothing like designing clothing. You have no right to tell me what I should or shouldn't be doing with my career."

"I have an obligation to speak up when I feel that another artist is doing a disservice to themselves."

"I'm not doing myself a disservice," I hiss. "Maybe you should focus on what you do best and let me focus on what I do best."

"What I do best?" he mimics me, his voice rising to a shrill pitch. "What exactly is that since you don't think I can write a book worth shit?"

"You're a genius at being an asshole." The sight of several women entering the store catches my eye. One is holding a large poster board with pictures of Nicholas attached. A hand-drawn heart surrounds one image of his face. "Your fan club is here, Mark Twain. I'll leave you to it."

"Mark Twain?" He smirks. "Cute, Sophia. They're not my fan club. I asked them to meet me here because the store closed last night before I could sign their books."

I thought I was safe coming to this bookstore since he spent hours here yesterday. This is the last place I expected to see him. "They're obviously eager. You should give them the attention they deserve."

"I'll have that book sent to your office tomorrow." He places both of the books in his hand back on the table. "I hope I'll run into you again, Sophia Reese."

I hate that he knows my name. I hate that he spent time researching me and that he found my website. I mostly hate that knowing that he's that interested in me makes me that much more interested in him.

Chapter 5

Nicholas

It took me less than five minutes to find out almost everything I need to know about Sophia Reese. After I had left the bistro with the full name of her boss, a quick online search revealed details about the fashion conglomerate he runs. A click through to the online profiles of the senior staff at Foster Enterprises steered me to a standard headshot of Sophia and a brief bio about her current position as assistant to Gabriel Foster and the business degree she earned at a community college in Florida.

Once I had her full name, I ran across the poorly designed website she uses to showcase her fashion designs. I wasn't lying to her when I said she has talent. She does.

"That's a new style for you, Nick. If I were you, I'd order it in light blue. It'll complement your eyes."

I flinch when I hear my younger brother's voice behind me. I'm sitting in his office, waiting for him so it shouldn't surprise me that he walked up behind me without me noticing. He's been doing that since we were kids. Years ago it would have ended with me in an inescapable headlock. Today, the result is that he caught a glimpse of my phone's screen and an image of the dress that I was looking at on Sophia's website.

"It's one-of-a-kind." I rub the bridge of my nose as my brother, Liam, passes in front of me. "It comes in yellow, take it or leave it."

"Yellow doesn't suit you." Liam tugs on the thigh of his jeans before he sits on the edge of his large wooden desk. "Who are you buying a dress for? Are you seeing someone?"

I glance up to see him smile. He's intimidating as fuck until you know him. He's burly, his hair a long textured mess of light brown and sun-kissed blonde. When I look at him, I still see the little kid who ran at my heel trying to gain my attention. I ignored him. Our older brother, Sebastian, did too. We didn't give Liam the time he deserved, but he turned out all right. He guides people through their grief now, helping them chart their future when a loss has taken away someone they loved.

"I'm not seeing anyone." I pocket my phone. "I met a woman on the subway. She's a fashion designer. I was checking out her stuff."

"Her stuff?" He crosses his arms over his chest. "Or her *stuff*?"

Considering I've only ever seen Sophia wrapped in a large white wool coat, her body is still a figment of my imagination. She's petite but curvy. Other than what the lines of her coat have given away, I have no idea what she's got hidden under it. I don't care. That face can stop traffic for miles.

"Grow up, Liam."

"I take it you struck out with her." He edges the toe of his boot against mine. "When's the last time that happened to you? It's got to sting."

I fucking hate when he's right. Since Liam became a therapist, it seems like he can read my mind. I try to keep a level mood when I'm around him, but he sees right through my bullshit. I hate it as much as I appreciate it. "I didn't strike out. We just met."

"You didn't try and lure her to that restaurant in the West Village by writing an invitation in one of your books, did you?" He squints at me. "Tell me you've stopped with that shit, Nick. It makes you look like a selfish fuck."

Generally, I don't care what I look like to the women I take to bed. I'll use my celebrity if I know it's going to result in a good time. The approach has never failed me, until now.

"Women like it, Wolf." I use his nickname to distract him. It always catches him off guard when he hears me say it. "I thought she'd show at the restaurant yesterday but she sent her boss instead."

He hesitates briefly, his eyes cast down as he absorbs what I just said. "You're trying to deflect. Don't."

"I'm not," I argue through a grin. "You're my Wolfie. You know it."

He ignores the comment in favor of focusing on my embarrassing lunch date yesterday. "Was the boss a he or a she?"

"A guy." I roll my eyes. "Gabriel Foster. He's a serious fan, so she sent him to meet me."

He chuckles. "Impressive. I like her already. What's her name?"

"Sophia," I say slowly, savoring the way it sounds. "Sophia Reese."

"Did you come here to talk about Sophia Reese? If you did, I'm all about that. I like a woman who knows what she wants. I guess in your case, it's what she doesn't want."

I shrug. "I'm not here because of her. I'm here to check in on you."

He scratches his elbow through the blue dress shirt he's wearing. "As you can see, I'm still in one piece."

"Are you?" I question with a tilt of my chin. "I know you deal with a lot of heavy shit all day, Liam. I'm around if you need an ear. You know that, right?"

"I can't talk about my clients with you, Nick." He arches his neck back. "Besides, I'm good. I'm helping folks who need me. What more could a guy want?"

"A life outside of this." I wave a hand at his desk and the stack of files sitting on it. "You're allowed to go out and enjoy yourself sometimes."

"I do." He flashes a quick grin. "I use your name to pick up women. It works like a charm every time."

I can't tell if he's kidding. "You do?"

"Shit no." He huffs out a deep laugh. "If a woman asks if I'm related to you, I tell her no. I can't compete with what you've got to offer."

I stand and extend my hand. "You're full of bullshit, Wolf."

He slaps my hand out of the way to pull me into a firm embrace. "If that's true I have you to thank for it. You and Sebastian taught me everything I know."

***

"Why are you here?" Sophia asks tersely as she rounds her desk.

I stare at her for a minute, taking in my first glimpse of her minus the oversized coat that's now hung on the coatrack behind her desk. Her long hair is styled in loose waves. She's wearing a red dress that's simple but elegant. The shoulders are cut bare to reveal her skin. "Did you design that dress?"

Her eyes brush over her body. "What? You didn't answer my question."

"Answer mine." I run my fingers over the spine of the book I'm holding in my hands. "Is that a dress that you designed?"

She takes a step back, her hip bumping into the corner of her desk. "Yes. Almost all of the clothes I wear, I've made. I design them and sew them."

"You sew them?" I glance down at the perfect hem of the dress. "You sewed this yourself?"

"Yes." Her eyes follow the same path as mine. "I've been sewing most of my clothes since I was in high school. I know what works for me. I'm an expert at creating things that fit me to a tee."

She sure as hell is. This dress clings to her like a glove. Her body is even more than I imagined it to be. Small tits, wide hips. She's ideal from head-to-toe.

"I answered your question, now answer mine. Why are you here?"

I push the book in my hands at her. "This is the new copy of *Burden's Proof* that I promised you last night."

She takes it from me, flipping open the cover to skim through the first few pages. A small smile ghosts her lips. "This one is good as new. I'll give it to Gabriel to replace the one you wrote in."

"I can sign it for him if you want," I offer without thinking. I know my signature is valuable currency. When I first saw signed copies of my books for sale online, I bought them.

Back then, I viewed it as a way to control my brand but I've learned that many people stand in line at my signings just for my signature. Once they've left the event, the book is sold with an inflated price tag. I've given up trying to curb that. It's the main reason I'll sign any book offered to me. If a fan of my work wants a personal piece of me in the form of a scribbled signature, I'll give it, freely and without question.

"You don't need to." She snaps the book shut. "You signed one book for him. I don't think he expects more than that."

"Who doesn't expect more?" Gabriel Foster steps out of his office and approaches us. "If you're talking about me, I'll take another signed book. If that is what you're offering, Mr. Wolf."

"Nicholas," I correct him. "Actually, I was offering to sign *Burden's Proof* for you."

He reaches past Sophia to pick up a blue ball point pen that's on her desk. "You can make this one out to me."

I take the pen and write a short inscription to him in the book before I finish it with my signature. "I should have signed this for Sophia on the day we met."

He takes the book from my hands. "I appreciate this but I've got to say that I'm surprised you came all the way down here to sign a book."

"I didn't." I turn to face Sophia. "I came down here to ask if you'd have dinner with me."

She looks at her boss before she trains her eyes squarely on my face. "When?"

"Tonight," I say without hesitation.

"I have plans." She pauses. "Unbreakable plans."

I drag my hand through my hair. "What about tomorrow night?"

"More plans," she says quickly. "I'm booked up for most of this year."

Gabriel clears his throat. "I'll leave you two alone to discuss this. Thanks again, Nicholas."

As he steps away I focus back on Sophia. "Are you seeing someone?"

"How is that your business?"

"Do you have a boyfriend?" I counter with a question of my own, trying hard to ignore the amused look on her face.

"I don't." She shakes her head. "I have a new maternity collection to work on and I can't spare any time to go out for dinner."

"I'll bring dinner to you," I hear myself say. Why do I sound so fucking desperate?

Her arms cross her chest. "I'm not telling you my address. You're a stranger."

"I'm not a stranger." I chuckle. "I'm not going to do anything other than bring you dinner, Sophia."

"I can make my own dinner." She moves back behind her desk. "I appreciate the offer, but I'm not interested, Mr. Wolf."

"Nicholas," I stress each syllable. "You are interested. We both know you are. Why pretend you're not?"

"I'm not pretending." She lowers into her chair. "I'm grateful you signed the books for Gabriel and Isla. Thank you again for that. You can go now."

"I can go now?" I repeat back. "Are you telling me to *fuck off*?"

Her brows pop up. "I didn't say that. If that's how you took it, I apologize but I have work to get to."

Jesus Christ. This woman isn't giving me an inch. I should turn around, walk out and forget she even exists.

I do the first, then the second and as I wait for the elevator to take me back to the lobby, I know that there's no way in hell I'm going to forget about Sophia Reese.

Chapter 6

Sophia

I try to avoid being rude at all costs. There's that old saying about catching more flies with honey than vinegar. It's something my mom used to repeat to me and my brother on an almost daily basis; that and the timeless jewel about not saying anything if you can't say something nice.

Nicholas was right. I was essentially telling him to fuck off but in a semi-polite way.

The man is dangerous. His smile says it all. It screams that he's a devil in bed and a monster in the afterglow. I don't need that. If I fall prey to his charms, my design schedule will suffer and I can't let that happen.

Men come and go in life, but my career is going to take me to the places I long to be.

It's as simple as that.

"Did you agree to have dinner with Nicholas?"

I've never once spoken to Mr. Foster about what I do when I leave my desk at the end of the day. He doesn't ask. I don't offer. It's an unspoken agreement between the two of us.

"What?" I look up and into his face. "Did you ask me about Nicholas, sir?"

"He invited you to dinner tonight and you turned him down. Did you find a night that works for both of you?"

Yes. It's the first Tuesday after the world ends.

"We didn't." I don't offer more; instead I bury my attention in a document that I should have filed a week ago.

"You have reservations about dating him, don't you?"

I'd rather have my fingernails pulled out with a set of pliers than have this conversation. "I'm not dating anyone right now. I'm taking a break from relationships."

I'm impressed with myself since that sounded borderline believable.

"Understood." Gabriel's gaze sweeps my desk. "I'm on the hunt for stock numbers for the new silk collection at Liore. Do you have those?"

I turn in my chair to open one of the file drawers behind me. "I have them right here, sir. I organized them by color to make it easier for you."

He takes the three file folders I hand him. "Excellent, Sophia. You're the most efficient assistant I've had. That means you're never permitted to quit. I hope you realize that."

I half-smile because I can't tell if he's joking or not. He pays me well including a significant raise just three months ago. The job is stable, he's a great boss and I'm done as soon as the clock strikes five o'clock but it's not enough. I'd eat ramen noodles at every meal for the rest of my life if it meant I had a chance to show my pieces at New York Fashion Week just once.

"I'll stick around for at least another week," I joke.

He raises a brow. "Make it two and I'll consider giving you one Friday afternoon a month off."

I brought up the subject briefly last week after I heard through the office grapevine that Gabriel's brother, Caleb, had given his assistant one day a month off with pay to spend with her toddler. I don't have children so when I mentioned the arrangement to Mr. Foster he promised me that if, or when, I become a mom, he'll afford me the same luxury. I left his office with a curse perched on my lips and a deep regret that I don't report directly to Caleb instead of Gabriel.

"Are you serious, sir?" I tilt my head to look up at him. "You're going to give me one afternoon a month off?"

"The last Friday afternoon of each month, Sophia."

"With pay?" I push because I need to. I spend as much as I can on my designs and every penny counts.

"With pay."

As tempted as I am to jump to my feet and hug him, I don't. Instead, I smile brightly. "Thank you, sir. You don't know how much this means to me."

"I suspect it means as much to you as those two signed Nicholas Wolf novels mean to me."

Nicholas Wolf. The brief time he spent in my life resulted in a nice perk in the form of extra time to devote to my passion. I should thank him, but that would mean I'd need to see him again and I have no intention of ever doing that.

***

As soon as I step out of the building at precisely five minutes after five, I tug on the collar of my coat to try and ward off the thick snowflakes that are whipping against the side of my face.

Snow was never part of my life back in Florida. I grew up in a small house with a seemingly happy mom and dad and an older brother who took me under his wing. My life has always been calm and controlled.

I've followed every rule laid out before me and I've taken the path of least resistance. My dream, when I was in high school, was to jet away the day after graduation for California. I pictured myself living on the beach and going to design school.

My parents didn't view that as a workable life plan, so they suggested, in a quietly controlling way, that I go to college in Florida and work toward a degree in business. I had no savings and no contacts in California, so I did what was expected of me.

Once graduation neared I started scouring job listings in both Los Angeles and New York. I landed an interview for an administrative job at a large company here in Manhattan. I nailed that and after working there for six months, I landed a position at Foster Enterprises. It was a junior assistant to one of the executives in merchandising. I used that as a means to my end goal. When I heard that Mr. Foster's assistant had quit, I marched up to his office, got myself in the door and spent an hour talking fashion with him. He offered me the job as his assistant on the spot.

"What time do you typically eat dinner? You're not one of those five o'clock people, are you?"

I turn instantly to my left at the sound of his voice. He's dressed as he was earlier when he came up to the office to drop off the book for Mr. Foster. Nicholas is wearing a black wool coat, jeans and now, he's sporting stylish black-rimmed glasses.

"Are you stalking me?" I slide my left hand into one of the tan leather gloves Cadence gave me for Christmas last year. "What are you doing here? I said *no* to dinner."

"I don't stalk anyone." His eyes fall to my hands. "I thought I'd give you another chance to say *yes*."

Another chance? He makes it sound as if I'm the one missing out.

"I don't need another chance. I don't want to have dinner with you."

"What about a drink?"

"No."

"Why not?"

Two women passing by us stop briefly to stare at him. The tall, blonder one, whispers something to her friend before they both shake their heads and move on.

"I'm not interested in you, Nicholas." I point after the women as they stroll toward the corner. "I bet either of those women would love to have a drink or dinner or maybe even both with you. If you hurry you can catch them before the light turns."

His gaze stays trained on my face. "I don't want to have drink or dinner with anyone but you."

"Why me?" I ask in exasperation. "I've said no already. Can't you just move on?"

"You need me, Sophia."

I laugh at the absurdity of that statement. "Your ego is the size of Texas. I don't need you."

"Your business needs me." He takes a step forward. "I was exactly like you once. I was posting chapters of my novels online hoping to find readers. I worked day and night to gain any ground I could. I was making mistakes that cost me time and money."

I eye him suspiciously. "You want me to have dinner with you so we can talk business?"

"Exactly," he says with a sharp nod. "That's it. It'll be shop talk, nothing else."

"You do realize that you write books and I design clothing?" I ask with a smirk. "You have no idea what it takes to make it in the fashion world."

He steps even closer as a group of people pass behind him. "I know how to create a personal brand that demands attention. That's what you need. It doesn't matter if it's books or dresses. Until you create a name for yourself, no one is going to notice your designs."

I finally slide my other glove on. "I'm not typically a five o'clock diner but I'll make an exception tonight. I'll give you an hour, Nicholas if you promise we'll talk business."

"Deal." He slides his finger along my chin. "You had a snowflake there."

I smile because the sudden snowstorm stopped the very minute we started talking.

Chapter 7

Nicholas

    I don't know how the fuck I ended up here. I'm not talking about this burger place less than two blocks from Sophia's office. I'm talking about how I wound up practically begging a woman I don't even know to have dinner with me. Technically, this isn't dinner in my book. I eat at eight or nine o'clock. The reason behind that is evident in this restaurant. The majority of the clientele is either under the age of ten-years-old or over the age of eighty.

    "How did you become famous?" Sophia asks before she sucks on the end of the straw that leads to the iced coffee she ordered.

    I stare at her mouth and those bright crimson lips. My cock isn't going to behave through this dinner and that's a problem. It's not because I mind rocking a hard-on in front of a beautiful woman. I don't. If that doesn't physically say, *I want you*, I don't know what does. The issue is the group of children sitting with their parents at the table next to us.

    "I wrote a good book," I answer without thinking. I get that I often sound like an egomaniac. I haven't always. There was a time when I was thrilled with the idea of anyone reading my work, but reality gets blurred when people start handing you checks with a lot of zeroes and women throw themselves at your feet.

I've tried to stay grounded but it's fucking hard when you're recognized almost everywhere you go and your bank account is a constant reminder of how many people crave your work.

"I design cute clothes," she counters with a smirk. "I'm asking how you got noticed, Nicholas? What did you do to get your work in front of the right people?"

The answer is simple, so I go with that. "I went back to the starting line."

"How so?" She sucks on the straw again, this time closing her eyes.

I cross my legs, willing my cock to calm the hell down. "I was sending out queries to agents for years. That started when I was in high school."

"I take it you had no success with that."

It's a fair assumption considering I only hit it big two years ago when I was twenty-six. "It was a waste of time. Years lost."

She nods like she gets it. I know she does. I checked out the time stamps on some of her older posts on her website. She's been designing clothing and uploading pictures of those items to her site for years. "When you stopped sending out queries, what did you do next?"

"Focused on college," I say quickly in response. "I went to school, studied writing and improved my craft."

"I've thought about taking a year off to go to design school, but I think I'm past that." She looks over at the kids next to us. "I see what the designers at Foster come up with on a daily basis."

"You think you're better than they are?"

Her eyes travel the length of the room before the settle back on my face. "I know that I am."

I smile. "Confidence is something I lacked after college. You've got it in spades, so you're ahead of the game."

"You weren't confident when you were twenty-four?"

"You're twenty-four?" There's no surprise in my tone. She looks young. I wouldn't have pegged her younger than she is, but it's obvious I have a few years on her. "I'm twenty-eight."

"I know." She taps the end of the straw with the pad of her index finger. "You weren't the only one searching for information online. I looked you up too."

I feel a rush of satisfaction knowing that. "What did you find?"

It's a question I instantly regret. I've stopped doing searches for my name because of all the shit that's unrelated to my work that's out there.

"Well," she drawls through a wide grin. "I found out that there are a lot of your books in Manhattan with lunch invitations written in them."

I sigh, looking at her face. "There's a few, Sophia. I wouldn't say there's a lot."

"I would." Her eyes brighten. "If it works for you, that's great. I happen to think it's a lame approach."

"No shit," I say before I clamp my hand over my mouth in response to a loud huff from the table next to us. "The swear police are on patrol."

"Little ears." She taps her earlobe causing the small silver earring to sway. "I'm trying to curse less.

My best friend is having a baby in a few months and I want to make a good impression on him."

She's too fucking sweet.

"Tell me where you see yourself in a year." I take a sip of the now tepid lemon water I ordered. "Where do you want your design business to be precisely a year from now?"

She hesitates briefly. "I want to be working for myself. I want my designs to be available in a retail setting… or, I want to be able to sell custom pieces from my website. Wait. I want both. I want to have both of those things in a year."

I don't point out the fact that she's not completely sure where she wants to be. I also don't mention that she has a lingering trace of the cream from her coffee on her bottom lip. "You can make both those things a reality if you set your mind to it."

"It's not as easy as wishing for it." Her gaze follows the server's movements as he places our meals in front of us.

I opted for a double cheeseburger and fries. Sophia chose a grilled chicken burger with a salad but it's impossible to ignore the way she's eyeing up my burger. "I want to taste the chicken so let's split our burgers. I'll take half of yours and you take half of mine."

"You want us to share?"

I don't want to share. I want her to myself even though we've barely spent thirty minutes in total together. "No, I don't want to share."

"You said you want to taste the chicken." She smiles as she pops a thinly sliced radish into her mouth. "You can have a bite if you want."

I shake my head and cross my legs tighter, my cock still not cooperating. "Give me half, Sophia. I'll give you half of mine."

"Deal," she says as he tongue glides over her bottom lip. "You're not as big of an asshole as I thought you were."

We both cringe when we hear the chorus of giggles next to us.

Chapter 8

Sophia

"Your burger was better than mine." I ball the paper napkin in my hand before I toss it onto my empty plate. "I don't eat beef that often, but that was too good for words."

He nods as he sips from his water glass. "I admit it was good. I typically head uptown when I want a burger. They make the best one at a place called Nova."

"I'll tell Tyler you said that the next time I see him," I say it as nonchalantly as I can manage. I'm not against dropping Cadence's name or that of her very famous fiancé. Tyler Monroe owns one of the most popular restaurants in the city. I eat there at least a couple of times a month and I've never paid a dime for a meal.

"You know Tyler Monroe?" He looks amused. "You mean you met him once when you were eating there, right? I did too."

"No." I sigh. "I actually know Tyler. My best friend is his fiancée."

I see the hesitation written all over his face. "Isn't his fiancée Cadence Sutton? She's on that morning show. I've caught her segment a few times."

"She's on Rise and Shine." I pause wondering if I should share more details or not. "Cadence and I lived together before she got engaged."

He leans back in his chair. "You have connections, Sophia. You should be using those to your advantage."

I know exactly what he means. He thinks I should send Cadence out into the world dressed in my designs. I would if she didn't have that ridiculous stipulation in her contract that requires her to wear Evlin's line. "Cadence can't wear any of my designs. She has to wear the brand that's specified in her contract when she's on air."

"Fair enough." He taps his long fingers against the edge of the table. "There must be another approach to take though. You have to be able to use your friendship with them to your advantage. They must know a hell of a lot of famous people."

"You're famous." I point out as the server clears our plates.

"I think it might damage my career if I parade around Manhattan in that tight yellow dress you call *Sunburst*."

"You saw that on my website." I feel a rush of color run over my cheeks. "You really did check it out, didn't you?"

"You need a better website." He ignores my question. "I have a guy who does mine. I can hook you up with him."

Every few months I give serious thought to revamping my site. I know exactly how I want it to look. I want it streamlined and simple with clickable links to my designs as well as a payment processor so if someone wants to order a piece, they can. Every quote I've ever gotten to change the site has surpassed my monthly salary at Foster Enterprises. I don't have the money to spare at the moment.

"I'm saving up for a better website."

He reaches to tug his phone from the front pocket of his jeans. The motion pulls the thin fabric of the navy blue sweater he's wearing taut across his chest. I already knew he was ripped based on those shirtless pictures of him online. I have to admit, he looks just as good in a sweater and jeans as he does half-nude.

"My guy has to update my site with a bunch of promo material for my next release." He scrolls through the contact list on his phone. "I pay him enough that he can take thirty minutes to look over your website. I'll get him to tweak it if you want. No charge."

I glance at his phone before I look back at his face. "I don't like being indebted to people. I'd want to pay him for his time."

He pushes his glasses up the bridge of his nose with his index finger. "Consider this a consultation. If you want to work with him after that, it's up to you. He'll work out a payment plan if that's better for you."

Wheels spin in my head. This is my chance to talk to an actual professional about my site for free. I may not be able to afford the changes he suggests, but I'll have a list of what I need to go on. I'd be an idiot not to take Nicholas up on his offer. "A consultation sounds great. Can I get his number?"

"I'd prefer to give him yours." He cradles his phone in his hand. "If you give it to me, I'll pass it on to him. It would be pretty hard to ask him for a favor for a friend if I don't even know that friend's number."

"You just want it so you can give it to him, right?" I eye him suspiciously. "You're not going to go all crazy stalker on me and send me messages in the middle of the night, are you?"

"I'm not as pathetic as you make me out to be." He smirks. "I'm passing your number on to Joe, my tech guy. I can't say that he won't send you messages in the middle of the night. He does his best work then."

I slowly call out each digit of my phone number as I watch him key it into his contact list wondering if I just made the best or worst decision of my life.

***

"Thanks for the burgers." I look past his shoulder and down the busy street where traffic is bumper-to-bumper. "I'm going to head home. I have a lot of work to do tonight."

"I'll grab us an Uber." He opens the app on his phone. "What's your address?"

"I live on the corner of None of Your Business and I'll Never Tell."

His head snaps up as he laughs. "Jesus, Sophia. I think we can both agree that I'm a fairly well-known guy. I'm not going to hang outside your building tossing pebbles up to your window so you can listen to me serenade you."

"You sing?" I ask teasingly. "Don't tell me that you can sing."

"Not a note." His finger hovers over his phone. "Can you?"

"No, but I play the piano," I confess. "I was classically trained."

"Are you any good?"

"I think I would have been accepted to Juilliard if I would have applied."

"And you say I'm the cocky one?" He mutters. "I have a piano at my place that I can't play. You should come over and tickle my ivories."

"You didn't just say that." I scrunch my nose. "That sounded like something…well, it didn't sound like you were talking about a piano."

"I wasn't." He finally closes the Uber app. "Look, if you ever want to come over to my place and play my piano, you're more than welcome. I'll keep my hands to myself. Scouts honor."

I watch as he raises his hand in the air. "You were a boy scout?"

"No." He sighs heavily. "Does that matter?"

I shield my smile with my gloved hand. "It doesn't matter. I can get home on my own. Thanks again for the dinner and the website contact."

"My pleasure." He steps toward me. "I'm going to kiss your cheek, Sophia, so don't knee me in the groin."

"I won't," I whisper as his soft lips brush against my skin.

Chapter 9

Nicholas

I wake with a start, the sheets around me a rumpled, twisted mess. I'm covered in sweat. The cold air that's enveloped the room from the slightly ajar window does nothing to cool me. I sit up, my mind still racing with the thoughts of the dream. It's the same fucking dream I have at least once a month.

I swing my legs over the side of my bed, taking in the lights of the city that usually offers me comfort. I can disappear in New York. When I stand and stare at the massive skyscrapers that punctuate the skyline, I feel invisible. During those brief moments, the haunting memories of my past dissipate. They don't consume me. They don't flood my mind with the thoughts that fuel my creative drive.

I couldn't write what I do if I hadn't lived through my past, yet it steals virtually every moment of my future from me.

That wasn't the case tonight when I had dinner with Sophia. She's right to be wary of me but not for the reasons she thinks.

I do want to fuck her. I don't know a man alive who wouldn't. She's beautiful and sensual, even if she doesn't realize it. When I leaned in to kiss her cheek, she sighed and her breath rushed over my chin. She smelled like spring, which feels eons away right now. She also smelled of the promise of a future that could be different.

I shake my head and pick up the water bottle I keep next to my bed. I swallow a large gulp, but it does nothing to calm me. I should get up and go for a run or take another shower. I had two since I left the restaurant.

The first was so I could jerk off and cleanse away the memory of Sophia. The second, an hour later, was cold as ice. It did little to quiet the hunger I still feel for her.

I scoop my phone into my palm and scroll through my contact list. I stop at her name, my thumb hanging over the screen above her number. It's past midnight. She'll be asleep by now in a bed I can't picture in an apartment on some nameless street on this island.

Unable to help myself, I reach out. I send her a quick text knowing she'll see it in the morning.

It's Nicholas. I'm texting to see if this is really you or if you gave me a fake number.

Her response comes almost instantaneously.

I knew you'd try and contact me in the middle of the night. Why are you awake? It's late.

I lean back on the bed and type out the first thing that comes to mind. It also happens to be the truth.

Bad dream.

At least a minute passes before I see the three dots jump that signal a reply.

I have a recurring dream about a duck. Don't ask but suffice to say I avoid the ponds at Central Park at all costs.

I laugh aloud as she types another message.

I'm going to sleep, Nicholas. I hope you were telling the truth about Joe.

I text back immediately.

I was. He'll be in touch soon, Sophia. Night.

I wait for a response, but there's nothing. I don't need it. I got her number and she didn't tell me to fuck off in her super sweet way. I'd call tonight a win.

***

"Once the book is released, your life will cease to be your own," Cheyenne, my publicist, points out as she scoops two spoons of sugar into her coffee. "You know the drill, Nick. Tour, television, podcasts, the works. I'm organizing your schedule now."

"You tell me where to be and I'm there." I sip my coffee.

"Is your brother tagging along this time?" She bats her eyelashes. "You know I have nothing against hanging out with Sebastian while you're hard at work."

I eye her over the rim of the mug before I place it back on the table. "Zeb has to work. He's staying here."

The last time I released a book my brother was due for a two week vacation from his position as a detective with the NYPD. He needed a break, so I dragged him with me to Europe for that leg of my tour. He had a blast although none of that happened with Cheyenne. She was married then. Now she's not and I don't have the heart to tell her that she's not Zeb's type.

"You could do a girl a favor and set us up, Nick."

"I'm doing you a favor by not setting you up with him." I tap my finger on the handle of the white ceramic mug that is a staple of this particular coffee chain. They serve Cheyenne's favorite blend so whenever she calls a meeting, this is our place. "You don't want to get involved with him. His life is his job."

"That's because he hasn't met the right woman yet." She tosses her long red hair over her shoulder. "I'm not easy to resist, Nick."

I've never had a problem resisting her. Cheyenne is a year older than me. She's attractive but our relationship mirrors the one I have with my sister. We fight like siblings, tease each other the same way best friends do. Hell, if I'm feeling sentimental I might consider jumping in front of a bus for her, but there's never been an ounce of sexual tension between us.

"I resist you just fine, Enne." I raise my mug in the air. "You're preaching to the wrong choir."

"I saw the way Sebastian looked at me. He was checking me out."

"He'd check out that empty chair if he walked in here right now." I point at a single wooden chair at the unoccupied table next to us. "He's a detective. He's always checking out everything."

"Way to rain on my parade, Nicholas." She narrows her eyes. "You must have friends you can set me up with. What about your other brother?"

"Liam is off limits." I shake my head, raising my hand in warning. "He's the baby of the family. You're too old for him."

"I'm perfect for him." She chuckles as she looks at two women taking a seat at a table a few feet from us. "I bet I could teach him a thing or two."

"Keep your panties on. My brothers are on your never-going-to-do list. Got it?"

"In that case, my sister is on your never-going-to-do-list."

I shrug. "You have a sister?"

"You're such a shit actor." She rolls her eyes. "You've been asking for my sister's number for the past year. Don't act like she doesn't exist."

I look at my watch. "A year? Why can't I remember her name or face at the moment?"

"God, you're such a bastard." She cups her hands over her mouth. "I don't care if you remember her or not, you are never putting one finger on my sister."

"Suits me fine," I reply with a smile. Unless her sister's name happens to be Sophia Reese I don't want my hands anywhere near her.

Chapter 10

Sophia

"How did that lunch go with the subway guy?" Cadence tugs on the hem of the white dress she's wearing. "This is too big for me. I think you made a mistake with the measurements."

"It's for the spring." I stand back and survey the way the fabric falls over her small stomach. "Once you're as big as a house, it's going to fit perfectly."

"I'm too tall to become as big as a house." She circles her arms in front of her as if she's imagines what her soon-to-be protruding belly will look like. "I've heard that tall women tend to show less and short women show more."

"That's wrong. My cousin, Marcie, is taller than you and boy, oh boy, she was enormous right before her son was born; enormous but beautiful."

"You're kidding." Cadence laughs as if her merriment is enough to prove my words wrong. "I'm already five months along. Look how tiny my belly is."

I purse my lips, tilting my head to the left. "You can't see it from this angle. I think tiny is the wrong word."

"Stop it." She cradles her stomach, her fingers splaying over the thin fabric of the dress. "We shouldn't be talking about this. We should be talking about you and Nick."

"I didn't go to lunch," I say knowing that it's deflecting from everything that's happened between Nicholas and me since. "I sent Mr. Foster in my place."

Her mouth quirks. "You sent your boss to have lunch with a man you met on the subway? Explain to me how that makes any sense at all."

There's no possible way I can continue this conversation without divulging exactly who I was supposed to meet for lunch. "I'll explain it if you promise you won't freak out over who the man on the subway is."

"What does that mean?" Cadence sits on the edge of my bed; her long legs stretched out in front of her. "Is he a criminal? Who the hell is this guy?"

"Promise, Den." I hold out my right pinky finger. "Pinky swear that you're not going to overreact to what I'm about to tell you."

"What are we eight years old now?" She wraps her finger around mine and gives it a firm tug. "I, Cadence Sutton, do pinky swear that I won't lose it when Sophia Reese tells me what the fuck is going on."

"I told you that I met that guy Nicholas on the way to a book signing," I remind her.

She nods her head enthusiastically. "We've established that. Move on."

"Fine," I snap back with a wide grin. "I was on my way to get a book signed for Mr. Foster. His wife asked me to do it as a favor for his birthday."

Her long finger taps the face of the watch on her wrist. "Time is wasting, Sophia. Why are you telling me where you were going? I don't care about the why, the where or even the when. I just want to know who the hell this Nick guy is."

I laugh and plop myself on the bed next to her. "I was on my way to get a book written by Nicholas Wolf signed."

I wait, hoping she's putting those two pieces together in her mind.

"What a weird coincidence." She shifts restlessly on the bed. "You were on your way to see a Nicholas when you met one."

I sigh in exasperation. I know she's tired. I get that she's been working her ass off, but Den is smarter than that. I spell it out in simple form for her. "I met Nicholas Wolf on the train on the way to his book signing."

She shoots me a look. "What? Sophia, what?"

"You heard me." I exhale wearily. "The man I met on the train is Nicholas Wolf. He was the guy I was supposed to meet for lunch, but I sent Mr. Foster in my place because Nicholas just wanted to sleep with me."

"So?"

"So?" I repeat back with a scowl. "You know I don't just sleep with any random guy. I won't and that's all he was after."

"Again, I'll ask, so?"

I can't help but laugh as I take to my feet to face her. "He's so sure of himself, Den. Like way too sure of himself. It drives me crazy. It's too much and since I keep saying no to him, he won't leave me alone."

"He's asked you to sleep with him?" Her brows rise. "Did he seriously ask if you wanted to fuck?"

I cover my face with my hands when I feel a rush of color invade my cheeks. "Not in so many words. When we were on the subway, he wrote down an address in the book I gave him to sign. It was a bistro in the West Village. He said if I showed he'd give me a copy of his next book. I planned on going until I went online and realized it's his signature pick-up move. He's done the same thing with other women before."

"It's original." Her gaze narrows. "I can't believe you stood Nicholas Wolf up and sent your boss in your place."

I wrinkle my nose. "I was scared that Mr. Foster would realize I sent him there blindly but he didn't. Nicholas didn't say a word about the fact that he had invited me there and not Gabriel."

"You dodged a bullet, Soph." She sets her hand on my shoulder. "The entire thing could have exploded in your face."

"I know," I murmur. "I'm lucky I still have a job."

"You said that Nicholas won't leave you alone, so I take it you've heard from him since you stood him up that day?"

I pause before I reply. "I've run into him a few times since then. He came to my office and then we ended up having a burger together last night."

"You went on a date with him after all?" She squeezes my shoulder through the thick denim shirt

I'm wearing. "You neglected to mention that you actually did said yes to him at least once."

I swat her hand away in jest. "We talked about my design business. He has a friend who is going to look over my website and tell me what I need to do to make improvements to it."

"So it was a business dinner, not a pleasure dinner?"

"Exactly," I say firmly. "We talked about websites, my designs and then we said goodnight."

"You like him, Soph." She jerks her thumb at me. "You smile when you talk about him."

"I don't." I wipe the back of my hand across my mouth. "I'm smiling because I'm talking to you."

"You're so full of it," she chides. "If you like him, give him a chance. What's the worst that can happen?"

"I'll feel like an idiot," I answer quickly. "Wait. No, I'll feel like a used idiot."

"Sex with a rock star in the literary world is not a bad thing. Besides, if he's still chasing you, maybe he's interested in more than that."

My gaze drifts to the stunning engagement ring on her left hand. Den was never a romantic before she met Tyler. That's all changed now that she's found her soul mate. She may want to believe that Nicholas sees me as more than a random fuck, but I know better. "I don't want to get hurt. I know how I am with men. If the sex is good, I'm going to be twirling in circles for weeks after when I stop hearing from him."

"You can't predict the future." She reaches for my hand. "If you like him, give him a chance, Soph. Maybe he'll surprise you."

Chapter 11

Nicholas

My cock is a bastard. Normally, I'd never think that. It's served me well. It's also served the women I've fucked well. Very well, in fact.

I love sex. I crave it. I'm aching to have it.

The last time I did was five days before I met Sophia. I went to a club in midtown and picked up a woman who had no idea who the fuck I am. She liked my face she said and an hour later in the cramped bedroom of her tiny walk-up in Hell's Kitchen, she screamed that she loved my cock as I was barrelling into her from behind. Natasha was the name she gave me. Apparently, it was part of the fantasy for her.

I saw her mail piled up on a small table next to the apartment door when I went to leave after she'd fallen asleep. Every envelope was addressed to the same person. Sherry Sinclair.

She'd dropped her clutch, phone, and keys on the table when we first walked in. Her hands were too busy trying to unbuckle my belt for her to notice the symphony of chimes that were signaling missed messages.

As I stood next to the table, I ordered an Uber to take me home and my eyes dropped to her phone as another chime filled the air.

The message that flashed across the screen was simple.

How was he, Sherry?

I smiled as I quietly exited the apartment I'd never set foot in again. If she answered whoever sent the message, truthfully she'd tell them the fuck was mind blowing. It was for her. It was at best average for me.

Average. It's always been average except for the first two times I made love. That was a lifetime ago and nothing's compared to that since.

I adjust my erection as I slide the zipper of the black trousers I'm wearing up. It's media day for me today. Cheyenne booked me a sit down with the host of one of the lifestyle shows that shoots in New York. She's taking a few weeks off which means she's pre-taping segments that will air during the month when *Action's Cause* is set to release.

After choosing a light blue sweater, I run some product through my hair. I glance down at my glasses on the bathroom counter but push them aside. I'm wearing contact lenses today, my preference most of the time, but too much time spent staring at the screen of my laptop tends to dictate that decision for me.

Not today though. I know how I want to look during the segment and I've nailed it. My hair is a deliberately styled mess, I haven't shaved in two days and the sweater matches my eye color. The majority of my fans are female. I give them what they want and that's the person I see reflected back in the mirror.

I'll turn on the charm for the interview, compliment the female host and by the time the segment does air, my book should be sitting pretty at the top of the charts.

***

"You're an incredible writer, Nicholas." Pamela, the host of the lifestyle show, touches my forearm with a little too much force. "Do you ever offer private readings? I bet if you did, the demand would be high."

Judging by the look in her eye, private readings is a euphemism for private fuck.

"I don't." I tug my arm free of her death grip. I had to do the same with my knee in the middle of our interview. "Once the book is released I'll be hosting public readings at several bookstores in the city. My publicist is the go-to for that."

Cheyenne waves as I turn to look at her.

"I've always wanted to write a book." Pamela wags her finger at me. "You'd be an incredible teacher. Will you mentor me?"

There's no way in hell that's going to happen. I can handle myself with virtually every woman I've ever met, but this one looks ready to pounce. She reminds me of my older sister, so that makes her completely off-limits.

"I don't offer mentorship." I smile as I scan the sparsely furnished studio space. There are bleachers that I assume are for the audience that typically views the taping of the show. Today, those are empty. "You're killing it at this job, Pam. This is a much better fit for you than the morning show."

"You remember me from Rise and Shine?" Her eyes widen. "I didn't realize that you were a fan, Nick."

I'm not. On the ride over, Cheyenne handed me a sheet of paper with ten pointers about Pamela. It's my publicist's way of breaking the ice. If I go into an interview prepared, I have more control. Today was no exception. I asked Pamela about her time spent in London where my first book was set and that helped her loosen up.

"I caught the show a few times," I segue smoothly. "I remember you had a great rapport with Cadence Sutton, the chef."

"Cadence?" She straightens her stance. "You're probably thinking of the connection between her fiancé, Tyler Monroe, and me. He had no problem teaching me a few things in the kitchen."

I squeeze my eyes shut to ward off the image of Pamela nude next to a hot stove.

"Cadence is a friend of a friend."

"Ah," she says on a sigh. "She's on set today. You should stop by and say hi, or I can introduce you."

I like food. I love meeting beautiful women. What possible harm can come from a simple introduction between Sophia's best friend and me?

Chapter 12

Sophia

"What the hell is this?" I look around the small restaurant eyeing every patron as I search for my best friend. "This doesn't make sense."

Nicholas is standing next to the table. The very same table that the hostess directed me to after I told her I was meeting someone for lunch. I specifically gave her the name the reservation was booked under. *Sutton.*

Since Cadence has been after me for weeks to try out this new vegan sandwich place, I agreed this morning through text. She told me to meet her here at noon sharp and that the reservation, for two, would be under her name.

It's been more than a week since I heard a peep from Nicholas. I thought he'd finally given up and although a small part of me wished he hadn't, I accepted it as fate. I had jotted down a note in my phone to find my own tech guy next week if I hadn't heard from Joe by then.

Now, I guess I can ask for Joe's number myself since Nicholas is my lunch date and not my best friend.

"Where's Cadence?" I cross my arms over my chest. "And why are you here?"

"Sit, Sophia." He rounds the table to pull on the back of the empty chair. "Please sit down and let me explain."

I catch a whiff of his cologne when he leans in to touch my arm. It's sophisticated and masculine and matches the way he looks today. He's dressed less casually, and more business-like in dark pants and a light blue sweater. "Don't touch me. I'm not sitting because I have no intention of staying. What have you done with Cadence? She's pregnant you know."

"You make it sound like I did something sinister to her." He wiggles his brows, his face mere inches from mine. "Cadence suggested I come. I met her this morning and she offered for me to take her place to have lunch with you."

"Cadence wouldn't do that to me," I say even though I know she would. Every day for the past week she's told me to reach out to Nicholas. I've complained about my schedule being too full and not having time to date, but her persistence hasn't waned.

Just this morning she told me that she'd force me to text him during lunch. It seems she decided to take action on her own.

"How did you meet her?" I take a deep breath to steady my pulse. "Did she call your publicist to get your number?"

His voice is even as he studies my face. "No, why would she do that?"

I purse my lips. "She's a fan of your work and I told her last week that we met."

"So you thought she was looking for an autograph or maybe another advance copy of *Action's Cause*?"

Or maybe she just wanted me to see him again.

Since we're running in a circle of confusion with no end in sight, I step on the brake and go for the truth. "No, Nicholas. Cadence thinks I should go out with you. I thought she contacted you to arrange this lunch."

"Really?" His cerulean blue eyes shine when he smiles. "I liked her the moment I met her. Now, I like her even more."

"You said you met her today?" I leave the question open-ended on purpose.

"I was uptown doing a pre-taped interview. Cadence happened to be in the same building in a different studio. The woman who interviewed me made the introduction."

I finally sit and wait for him to do the same before I speak. "You're telling me that you just happened to be at the Rise and Shine studios this morning?"

"Pamela, the host of the show I did the interview for, used to work with Cadence."

"I've met Pamela," I say in a soft voice. "It's a small world."

"Manhattan is a small place," he affirms. "I was glad to meet her. Chef Sutton is very talented."

I nod, my eyes flicking to his face. "She is. She's an incredible cook."

"It was her idea for me to meet you here for lunch, Sophia." He waves the approaching server away with a dismissive hand. "If you'd rather I leave, I will, but I'd prefer to stay."

Cadence set me up. She put me in the very same position I put Mr. Foster in. The glaring difference is that I know why she did it and I'm grateful. "Stay. It's not every day I get to eat vegan with the one and only Nicholas Wolf."

***

"How does a person realize they can write novels about police detectives?" I ask after I swallow the last bite of the salad I ordered.

Nicholas had finished his grilled vegetable and pesto sandwich before I was half done. Since then he's sat and watched me eat while asking generic questions about my time spent in Florida.

"My father is retired NYPD. My brother works in homicide. It fit for me to write about it."

I lean my elbows on the table on either side of my plate. "Do you base your books on actual cases?"

He motions for the server standing nearby to clear our plates. "I go to my dad or my brother if I have a general question but neither has ever offered specifics about a case. I don't ask. It's understood that what happens at work stays there."

That's the reply I expected. When I was a child, the man who lived next door to us was a police officer. His job and his family were his life. He was a hero to me and whenever I saw him come home from work dressed in his uniform, I'd feel enormous respect and reverence. I might not have completely understood the sacrifices police officers make back then, but I did know that he was special.

"Is it hard writing about death?" I blurt that out just as the server reaches for my plate. He hesitates briefly before he clears all the dishes.

"Death is only the beginning of the story. Understanding why the death happened is the part that can be challenging."

"You're the author." I look down at my watch. "If you don't know why the death happened, who does?"

"You have eight minutes before you need to be back." He points at the large silver watch on his wrist. "Your office is three minutes away if you walk briskly that means I have exactly five more minutes with you."

"Eight if you walk me back to the office."

His smile is cocky. "At least thirty if I come up with you and say hello to Gabe."

"Gabriel," I say curtly. "He hates it when anyone calls him Gabe. His brother does it and it never ends well."

"Gabe it is." He stands and reaches for my coat that I'd slung over the back of an empty chair next to us. "I'll bet you dinner tomorrow evening that if I call him Gabe, he'll just nod and smile."

"Dinner tomorrow?" I stand and turn my back to him so he can help me with my coat. "As in, we have dinner if he nods and smiles and we don't have dinner if he gets pissed?"

"No." His fingertips brush the skin at the back of my neck as he gently tugs my hair out from beneath the collar of my coat. "If he nods and smiles, you'll let me cook for you and if he gets pissed, you'll cook for me."

A shiver of excitement races up my spine when I turn sharply to face him. "That's a serious wager."

"If you're not sure you can win, I understand."

Cadence's words about giving him a chance echo through my mind. I know I'll lose the bet. Mr. Foster will likely adopt the nickname *Gabe* if his favorite novelist calls him that. He won't get pissed, that I know for sure.

"You have a bet." I hold out my hand. "Dinner tomorrow it is."

He wraps his hand around mine and raises it to his mouth. His soft lips trace a path over my palm just as he leans in and whispers, "I can't wait to cook for you tomorrow."

Chapter 13

Nicholas

"You didn't complain about the menu, Sophia." I hold back a smile. "Thank you for that."

She skims a white linen napkin over her mouth. "Tomato soup and grilled cheese sandwiches are two of my favorite things. It was snowing on my way over, so I can't think of anything more perfect to eat on a night like tonight."

You. You'd be perfect to eat on a night like tonight.

"I made the soup from scratch." I look over my shoulder at the mountain of dishes in the sink. "I want you to know that I didn't just open a can of soup and pour it into a pot."

Her gaze follows mine and she visibly cringes at the sight of the work she thinks I have ahead of me. I won't be touching a single dirty dish. I'll leave them until tomorrow when the cleaning staff I hired comes in for one of their twice weekly visits. They'll have the kitchen looking like polished perfection within an hour. "I can help with those, Nicholas. I have lots of experience washing dishes."

"It would be a crime to wash dishes in that dress." I take a swallow of the wine she brought with her. Surprisingly, it pairs perfectly with our modest meal. "If you're offering to do them in the nude, the dish soap is under the sink."

A blush sprints up her slender neck to her cheeks. "I don't wash dishes in the nude."

"There's a first time for everything."

The tip of her tongue slicks her bottom lip as her gaze drops to the emerald green sheath dress she's wearing. "I'll skip the dishes."

"Fair enough." I pour more wine into both our glasses. "I saw you eyeing the piano before dinner. I'd love a private concert."

She had stopped to run her index finger along the keys shortly after I invited her in. I'd texted her earlier, offering to send a car to pick her up but she was adamant about coming here on her own. I gave her my address and paced my apartment for an hour before she finally texted me to say she was in the lobby. Once she was at my door and I took her coat, I saw the tension in her shoulders. She's relaxed now, but her guard is still up. That's evident in the way her knee high black boots are tapping a rhythmic beat on the hardwood floor.

"I haven't played in a while." She sets her elbow on the table. "I think I could manage a little something."

I'll take anything I can get. I want her to feel at ease. "Whenever you're ready, the piano is all yours."

"I wish," she says as she stands. "A piano is the first thing on my list when I make it big in the fashion world. No, wait, it's the second. First, I'll get a place of my own that overlooks the city and then I'll buy a piano that I'll put right in front of the window so I can look out at New York while I play."

I have both of those things now and can't say that I appreciate either that much. The piano came with the apartment. I'd debated having it carted out after I moved in, but it brings a touch of sophistication to the space that I like. My brothers keep telling me that it's a waste to have it here, but I've never viewed it that way. It's a reminder of the summer I took piano lessons when I was ten-years-old. It's the only thing I've ever quit. One day I'll take it up again and prove to myself that my dad's words about reaching and attaining the impossible are true. I just need to get my fingers to cooperate.

"So you've never learned how to play?" She motions toward the main room where the piano is. "How can you not when you have that staring you in the face every day?"

"I'd like to learn," I say as I watch the sway of her ass as she walks through my apartment. "Maybe you can teach me sometime."

"I'm a horrible teacher." She looks back over her shoulder at me, a mischievous glint in her eye. "I don't have the patience. I wish I did."

"We could do a trial run." I inch up behind her as she stands next to the baby grand piano. "One lesson and if I'm hopeless, you'll give up."

"I'll consider it." She touches the bench in front of the piano. "May I?"

"Please." I study her profile as she sits in place, the hem of her dress tucked under her knees.

"This piano is exquisite." She runs her finger along the gentle curve of the music rack. "The one I used to play back home in Florida looked like it came out of a saloon from the 1920s."

I stop mid-sip of my wine to laugh. "Why can I picture that?"

She laughs, her gaze still riveted to the keys. "It was like it belonged on the set of an old western movie. It was never tuned properly so I did the best I could. My music teacher had the piano of my dreams, or so I thought until today."

"You can come over and play this one whenever you want." I deliberately keep my tone light. "I'm not one to turn down a private performance by my favorite dress designer."

"Let's see how my debut goes and then we'll talk." She flips her head back to look into my eyes. "Promise you won't laugh if I'm rusty."

"I can't play a note, Sophia." I raise my glass in the air. "I assure you that laughing is the last thing I'll do once you start."

Her top teeth grab hold of her bottom lip and the only thing I want is to feel that for myself. I haven't pushed her even though I've wanted to kiss those red lipstick stained lips since the first moment I saw her on the subway. I've surprised myself with the level of restraint I'm showing. My resolve is weakening though, especially since we're alone in my apartment and her nipples are now visibly hard points beneath the thin fabric of the dress she's wearing.

"I need to warm up. Cover your ears while I do that."

I place the wine glass on the piano and do as I'm told.

She stares at me for a long minute before she bursts out laughing. "I was joking."

"Jesus," I mutter under my breath. "You can make me do anything."

"Anything?" Her left brow perks. "I'm going to test that theory."

"Tonight?" I ask. I take a deep breath before I continue because I know the words I'm about to say come with a risk. She could walk the hell out of here and never look back or she could stay and contemplate the possibility of something developing between us. "Say you'll test it tonight, Sophia, because I promise if you asked me to do anything to you, I would."

There's no blush this time, her eyes don't leave mine. Instead she swallows hard and then, finally, turns back to the piano. "Sit and listen, Nicholas. Just relax and let the music flow through you."

Chapter 14

Sophia

I took an entire three minutes to debate what I'd play for him. Typically, when someone asks me to play the piano, I'll dive into the easiest song I know; Mozart's *Moonlight Sonata*. I can play it with my eyes closed but I didn't want to revert to the familiar. Instead, I chose Schumann's *Arabeske*. It's a piece I struggled with for more than three months before I finally perfected it in my senior year of high school.

As I finished the last note and opened my eyes, I turned to see Nicholas sitting in a leather chair less than a foot away, his eyes glued to my hands.

"Sophia," he whispers now, a full thirty seconds after I regrettably took my fingers from the keys. "That was breathtaking. I don't think I've ever heard anything more beautiful."

It was good. The music flowed through me. It didn't hurt that this piano is tuned to perfection. My impulse is to play another song and then another. I could literally sit here all night and savor the sound of this beautiful instrument.

"Your piano is magnificent." I stare at the open lid. "If I had it, I'd never be able to tear myself away from it. This is my addiction."

"I can see why." He taps his earlobe. "I can hear why. You have a gift for this. You must know how incredible you are."

I blush, but it's not from the compliment. It's from the look on his face. He's mesmerized. My first piano teacher would repeat during each of my lessons that my goal was to captivate those who heard me play. I'd search for that certain look in the eyes of the people who came to my recitals. I didn't see it at first, but as my body learned to appreciate and master the music, I began to see it more and more.

"I know that I'm good," I admit without faltering. "I could have been better if I'd have chosen to pursue this."

"Why didn't you? Was it because you wanted to design clothing?"

That's obviously part of it. The other is that my parents didn't see a sustainable future for me as a professional pianist. I didn't either. I never wanted my passion to play to morph into an obligation. I play because it brings me inner peace, not because I'm dependent on it for a paycheck.

"I love designing more than I love playing." I turn on the bench so I'm facing him. "At one time my heart was split in two but I want to see my designs on people. I play the piano for a different reason than I design. Playing fuels the creative part of me and designing is the outlet."

"They go hand-in-hand." He clasps his hands together before he steeples his index fingers to bring them to his lips, his elbows resting on his knees. "When's the last time you played?"

"There used to be an independent music store a block from my apartment." I place my hands in my lap. "I'd stop there at least a few times a week on my way home from work to play. The owner didn't mind.

When he decided to close his shop last summer he asked if I wanted to buy the piano, but I couldn't afford it."

His shoulders lower as his hands tense. "I told you earlier that you can stop by to play this one whenever you want. I meant that."

It's a generous offer that I'm seriously considering. Not only would it give me a chance to play, but it would mean more time spent with him. I'm beginning to wonder if I misjudged him. He looks at me like he wants to eat me up, but his words and his actions are restrained. He's not rushing me into something I may not be ready for and for that I'm grateful.

"Maybe we can work out a schedule for visitation," I joke.

"That discussion needs to include details about what the visitation will cost you."

The air around me suddenly feels much thicker. I've been hyperaware of everything about him since I arrived. That's not surprising given how he's dressed. It's all black, from the trousers to the button down shirt. The only color that's visible on him is his eyes. Each time I see them, I'm amazed at how strikingly blue they are. Mine pale in comparison to his.

I don't back down from his statement. It might be the faint buzz I feel from the glass of cheap wine I had with dinner. It could be the rush I experienced from playing such a difficult piece so effortlessly. Whatever it is it fuels me to look him straight in the eye. "Is the price steep?"

"It's manageable."

I feel my face heat. "How do you know it's manageable for me?"

"You've kissed a man before, Sophia. We'll start there."

"A kiss?" The words catch in my throat. It's not as if I've never been kissed. I have by plenty of men. I remember some of those kisses with a longing that's faint but familiar like the smell of rain in the distance after a long drought. I can't recall the taste of the lips or the names of the others. Those are the men I didn't share my body with because their kiss wasn't enough to make me wonder what it would be like to taste more.

He leans forward on his elbows, his hands parting. "You want to kiss me. You have since we met."

"No, I haven't," I say with conviction even though I know it's not the truth.

"You're a liar." He stands and faces me. "Give me your hand."

I stare at his outstretched hand for a heartbeat. The skin is smooth, the lines that cross his palms faint. My gaze follows the path of his skin up the sleeve of his shirt that covers his muscular forearm and bicep before it lands on his face. "Just a kiss, Nicholas?"

"One kiss." His fingers curl in unison, beckoning me to take his hand.

I place my hand in his knowing that I can't turn back. I don't want to. I want to kiss him. Hell, I want so much more. He's every woman's dream. His black hair is a tousled mess. The subtle shading on his jaw gives him an edge that promises of a hint of roughness. His lips are full and pink. They're the most kissable lips I've ever seen on a man and he's right. I've wanted to kiss him since the moment I turned to look at him on the subway.

"Come here," he whispers darkly as he tugs me to my feet.

I don't resist when he rests my hand on his chest over his beating heart. His pulse is racing and his breathing is shallow. If I didn't know better, I would think that he's as nervous about our first kiss as I am.

I don't say anything when his hand slides up my arm to the back of my neck. I draw in a deep breath when he tilts my head and looks into my eyes. I smile at him before he bites his bottom lip.

"You're beautiful, Sophia," he says in a husky voice. "I've never met anyone like you."

I close my eyes just as I feel his lips touch mine.

Chapter 15

Nicholas

I take my time with the kiss. My first taste of her is better than I imagined and when I slide my tongue along the seam of her lips and she opens herself to me, she moans. It's soft, almost inaudible, but I hear it. I feel it reverberate through our kiss.

I tighten my grip on her neck as my other hand circles her waist. I pull her closer, wanting to meld her body with mine. I know she can feel my arousal. My dick is hard as concrete, aching to be inside of her.

Her hands grip the front of my shirt, the material fisted in her palms. She tugs slightly as if she wants us closer. She needs more and I'm not about to deny her anything.

I slide my hand lower until I'm cupping that delectable ass. It's soft and lush beneath her dress. "Sophia." I breathe the word into our kiss. "Please."

She shakes her head slightly just as she deepens the kiss. Her tongue glides against mine in a silent invitation to take more. So I do.

I move my hand lower until it skims the hem of her dress. I want to touch the flesh of that beautiful ass and run my fingers between her legs. I need to feel her wetness. I have to know that she craves me too.

"Nicholas." Her voice is a whisper as she pulls back. "Just a kiss tonight."

I want more. I need it, but I'm not the type of guy to push when a woman pulls back. I won't do it. I break the kiss, my hands loosening their grip.

"You can really kiss." She leans her forehead against my chin. "Like holy fuck, you can kiss."

I laugh deeply. "I'd say the same for you."

Her eyes are cast down. They're in perfect alignment with the outline of my massive erection through my pants. She has to know what she's doing to me; what she's done to me since the first night we met.

"I need a cold shower," I say half-jokingly. "That or a nude run in the snow."

"A nude run in the snow?" Her head pops us to look at me. "No one does that."

"I did it once," I say with a straight face. "You're welcome to join me the next time I do it."

She studies me carefully. "I'm not as gullible as you. I don't fall for things that easily. You've never run around New York in the nude."

"You think I'm gullible?" I ask on a grin. My eyes are glued to her mouth and the faint trace of red lipstick that's still there.

I want that mouth on my dick. If she blows cock the way she kisses, I'll lose it within the first minute.

"You fell for it when I told you to cover your ears before I started playing your piano." She raises her hands to her ears. "I'd call that gullible."

"I'd call it being a gentleman. I'm guessing you're not used to that."

Her hands drop to her hips. "You consider yourself a gentleman?"

I toss her a condescending smile. "Absolutely."

She throws her head back in laughter. "You were groping my ass when we were kissing. I'm pretty sure you're not going to find ass groping listed as one of the definitions of the word *gentleman* in the dictionary."

"That thing is a magnet for these." I wave my hands in the air in a wide arc. "You have the best ass I've ever seen. I'm saying that in the most gentlemanly way I can."

She looks over her shoulder as if she expects to catch a glimpse of her spectacular ass. "You like it?"

"What do you think?" I adjust the buckle of my belt in an effort to pull her gaze down to the outline of my erection through my pants. "You have to know what you're doing to me."

"I know." She keeps her eyes trained on my face. "I felt it. That's biology though. You can't help it. It probably happens whenever you see a woman's ass."

"I'm not sixteen-years-old." I lean in closer. "I want you. That's why my body is reacting like this. I want to strip you naked and carry you to my bed. I want to taste you, touch you and yes, Ms. Reese, I want to fuck you."

Her lips open until her mouth is a perfect O.

"This game we've been playing has been fun," I go on. "I'll continue for as long as it takes but one day soon I need to be inside of you. I know you want the same thing."

She swallows, her gaze moving from my face to the front of my pants before her eyes meet mine. "You don't know what I want. You can't read my mind, Nicholas."

"You're right. I can't read your mind." I pause. "I can sense that you want me though. You can pretend that it's not real, but if you do that, you're just lying to us both."

She stands her ground, listening to every word I'm saying. "You don't know me. You're basing all of this on your experiences with other women. I bet you're used to women fawning all over you. You think that just because most women will bow at your feet, that I will too."

"You're wrong," I say succinctly. "This has nothing to do with other women."

She steps back, her shoulders tense again. "I doubt like hell that you've ever had to put in any real effort to get a woman into bed. When's the last time you chased a woman?"

I move to lessen the distance between us but she counters with another step back. "Do you want me to chase you, Sophia?"

"I didn't say that." Her hand darts in the air to stop me in place. "Besides, I'm not sure you could ever catch me."

"Is that so? Because from what I've seen…" I begin as I run my index finger along the curve of her chin. "I'm not sure you can handle what's going to happen once I do catch you."

"I can handle it," she whispers under her breath before she moves away from my touch.

"What was that?" My gaze narrows. "I missed that."

She shoots me a look. "I said I need to go home."

"That's not what you said."

Her mouth twists ruefully. "I'm leaving. This has been interesting."

"I'll say," I quip as I tug my phone from the front pocket of my pants. "I'll call for a car. Don't worry. I won't follow behind in the shadows."

"I know you won't," she says, her voice a more even tone. "You're not up to the chase."

"Challenge accepted." I look her dead in the eye. "I want you, Sophia. Don't expect me to give up easily."

A small smile ghosts her lips. "Surprise me, then, Nicholas. Prove me wrong."

"I intend to." I lean forward to kiss her forehead. "I'm a better man than you think I am. I'm also persistent when I see something I want."

She opens her mouth to say something but I stop her with a quick kiss to her lips.

"I'll give you a head start." I move to grab her coat from the chair I placed it on when she arrived. "Then the chase is on."

"You seriously think you can catch me?"

I move behind her to help her with her coat. "I will catch you. This thing between us is too strong to ignore. We will happen. Mark my words."

She turns quickly on her heel, her eyes raking me from head-to-toe. "We'll see. I'll find my own way home tonight."

With that she scoops up her purse, tosses her hair behind her shoulders and walks out of my apartment without a single glance back.

Chapter 16

Sophia

I admit that I want him to work for it, even if it's just a little bit. I was tempted to give in when Nicholas was kissing me. My body was screaming at me to let him inch his fingers up the skirt of my dress so he could feel my arousal, but I stopped it. I had to. If I would have slept with him last night, I doubt I'd be sitting at my desk now staring at the dozen light violet roses that were delivered this morning.

I knew instantly that they were from him. I didn't even have to open the card that was attached to the bouquet, but I did.

Thank you for last night, Sophia. Nicholas. xx

"Those are beautiful." Gabriel stops at my desk on his way into his office. "Would it be out of line if I asked if those were from Nicholas Wolf?"

It wouldn't be. Our relationship has slowly morphed from being strictly business to having faint touches of friendship woven into it. It's the main reason I agreed to go to the book signing when Isla, Gabriel's wife, asked me to. She told me that she planned to go herself but Gabriel's brothers Caleb and Asher decided to throw him a pre-birthday surprise dinner party. She had to be there, so I ventured out to the signing in her place.

I may have to thank her for that since that's the night I met Nicholas.

"They're from him." I tuck the card into my palm to shield the words from Gabriel's view.

He bends down to smell one of the perfectly symmetrical blossoms. "He has excellent taste in flowers and women."

The compliment is unexpected and I fumble in my mind with what to say in response. "Thank you, sir."

"Tomorrow is the last Friday of the month, Sophia." He stands upright, his left hand reaching to adjust the lapel of his jacket. "That means you can leave at noon for the weekend."

I've kept a close eye on the calendar and on Mr. Foster to see if he'd remember the promise he made. "Thank you again. It's with pay, right?"

"That it is."

I nod as he turns to walk back toward his office. When he's completely out of view, I fish my phone from the purse hanging on the coatrack near my desk. I open it and scroll through my contact list until I land on his name. Then I type out a quick text message.

The flowers are beautiful, Nicholas. Thank you.

I reach to drop my phone back into my purse when I hear the faint chime that signals a new message.

They pale in comparison to you. (Cheesy, I know.) Do you want to play the piano tomorrow? Say at seven?

I bite my bottom lip while I consider the invitation. I told him I wanted him to chase me and he is but if I walk back into that apartment so soon, I know I'll end up beneath him in his bed. Besides, I do have somewhere I need to be tomorrow night.

I type back a response, keeping one eye on the open door of Mr. Foster's office.

I have plans tomorrow. Maybe one night next week?

A boulder forms in my stomach as I watch the three dots jump as he types.

Next week it is. I'll be in touch.

I stare at the screen, reading the message twice. I expected him to suggest another day when I turned him down, but he didn't. I shrug it off, toss my phone back in my purse and get to work emailing all Foster executives about the board meeting next Tuesday.

***

When I open the door to my apartment the next afternoon, I'm surprised to find not only my best friend standing behind the stove but a stack of bridal magazines on the counter next to her.

"Den?" I say her name loud enough that she'll hear me over the buzz of the exhaust fan that is on its highest setting. "What are you doing here?"

It's a question I always hate asking when she shows up unexpectedly. She owns this two bedroom apartment outright so I can't exactly ask for her keys back. I appreciate the company on most days, but today I had a clear plan in place. I want to finish the white maternity dress I started last week before I need to leave at seven o'clock. I had every intention of dropping by Den's place tomorrow to give it to her and get her to model it for me so I can upload images of it to my website.

"This is your first official, Friday afternoon off, so I'm here to celebrate." She waves her hand through the smoke that's billowing off the two pieces of salmon she has on the indoor grill. "We're having salmon with that grainy mustard sauce you love and a sauerkraut salad with a mayonnaise dressing."

I cringe inwardly. The salmon sounds delectable. The sauerkraut salad seems more like a weird pregnancy craving than something I'd want to voluntarily eat.

"You didn't have to do this," I say gently. "I'm not that hungry."

I'm famished. I skipped breakfast entirely because I was hand sewing pearls on the white dress right after I woke up. I picked up a small coffee at the bodega on the corner but ended up tossing it in a trash can before I stepped on the bus. It was bitter and obviously left over from yesterday.

"I'm starving." She rubs her stomach. "Firi is a food fiend. My boy is always hungry."

I feel tears instantly well in my eyes. "Is that the baby's name?"

The fork that was in her hand drops to the counter before it bounces to the floor. "Tyler wants to name him after my dad. I love it, Soph. He'll be little Firi Monroe."

I love it too. Cadence has worked hard for the past year to bridge the emotional gap that developed between her and her dad, Sergio Firi. She may have followed in his footsteps when she became a chef, but that didn't cement their relationship. They were estranged for years and now, finally, they've found their way back to each other.

"It's perfect, Den." I wipe my eyes with the back of my hand. "He's going to be the most amazing little boy in the world."

"You and I both know it." She smiles proudly. "I can't wait for him to get here. I want you there, Soph. I'm going to need you with Tyler and me in the delivery room when he's born."

I reach to grab hold of her forearm to steady myself. The rush of emotions I feel barrels through me like a freight train. "I'll be there. I wouldn't miss that for the world."

"Good." She brushes her lips across my forehead. "I want you to kick off your shoes, change out of your work clothes and get ready for a meal you'll never forget."

I turn to race to my bathroom where I keep the antacid in the medicine cabinet. I might as well nip the indigestion I know is coming in the bud.

Chapter 17

Sophia

I ate the salmon first and now as I pick at the sauerkraut salad, I stare across the room at the roses that Nicholas sent to me. I'd brought them home yesterday after work. Lugging the heavy vase and flowers on the subway wasn't an easy task. I'd carefully wrapped them in the packaging they'd arrived in and after considering hailing a taxi outside my office building, I decided that the subway would work just fine. My stop is less than a block from my apartment, so I made it home with the vase still in one piece.

"Nicholas Wolf sent you those," Cadence says matter-of-factly. "I noticed them when I came in. I hope you don't mind that I read the card."

I don't mind. Why would I? I had every intention of telling Den that I had dinner with Nicholas at his place. I was going to tell her when we first sat down to eat lunch but she'd started talking about her wedding and hadn't stopped. The only time she wasn't speaking was when she was chewing.

"I had dinner at his place." I place my fork on my plate. "He made me tomato soup and grilled cheese sandwiches."

She uses both hands to seamlessly switch our plates by sliding mine in front of her and vice versa. She reaches over to grab her fork from the empty plate that's now in front of me. "I'm going to finish this if you don't mind."

I'm grateful that she's offering to eat it. The salad brought tears to my eyes when I took that first bite. It wasn't because I hated the taste, even though I strongly disliked it. The heavy dose of vinegar in it made my toes curl. "It's all yours."

"It's adorable that he cooked for you, Soph." She bats her eyelashes. "He's crushing on you, isn't he? Do you feel the same way about him?"

I owe it to Den to be honest. She's always been with me, even when her relationship with Tyler was confusing, she confided in me how she felt. I knew she was in love with him before he did. "I like him. There's something about him that I really like, Cadence."

"Don't sound so cheery about it," she jokes on a smile. "You're frowning, Soph. You look miserable. If you like him and he likes you, what's the problem?"

She knows my dating history. I've never gotten close enough to any man to even consider marriage, but I did love someone once. His name was Jeremiah. I met him during my second year of college. He was an associate professor and although he never taught me in the classroom, the lessons he left me with have been long lasting.

I was drawn to him because of who he was around campus. He was bold and sexy. His approach to teaching was aggressive. He was granted tenure at just thirty-years-old and during the months before we broke up, he invested almost every waking minute working on a short film. It was a documentary, about

99

repressed memories, a subject he'd always been fascinated with.

After the film's local release in Florida, it caught the attention of people nationwide. With every compliment and rave review he received, his interest in me waned until he finally dumped me on a rainy Wednesday night because he thought our relationship was impeding his pending fame. The entire experience left me with a bitter taste in mouth.

"What if he ends up being like Jeremiah?" I ask aloud, even though I know the question has no merit. Nicholas has already found fame and fortune. That part of his life is firmly in place and what we're nurturing doesn't hinge on his success.

She scoops the last bite of salad in her mouth and chews. Her eyes stay trained on my face until she swallows. "You know I dated that idiot Brendon before I met Tyler. They're both chefs, but that's where the similarities end. If I would have had a no dating chefs rule, I never would have fallen in love with Tyler and little Firi wouldn't exist."

I know that punishing Nicholas for a brief failed relationship in my past is wrong. It's not his fault that I once fell in love with another creative person. "Tyler's pretty cocky, isn't he?"

"Very cocky." She rolls her eyes. "He has every right to be. He's a wizard in the kitchen. I'm amazed by his talent.

"Does it ever bother you?"

"That he's cocky?" she asks with a chuckle. "It used to but I realized that I'm insanely attracted to that part of him. I love that he gets how good he is. He owns it. It's hot."

It is hot. The more I learn about Nicholas, the more I see that he's proud of his gift. He doesn't shy away from the fact that he's built an empire that has essentially been born from his own thoughts. It's an accomplishment that not many men can stake claim to.

"I don't want him to hurt me, Den." I shake my head. "He's the kind of guy I could fall hard for."

She moves both our plates aside before she reaches for my hands. "I know it's not easy to just put yourself out there but if you like him, I think it's worth the risk."

"Will you come over and console me when he dumps me?"

"I will," she concedes. "For the record, I don't see that happening. You're strong, Sophia. Give yourself some credit. You can let yourself feel things and if it doesn't work out between you two, it won't destroy you. You still have me and you'll always be a kick ass designer."

I know she's right. I'm stronger than I was when Jeremiah ended our relationship. I can let myself feel things with Nicholas and if it all goes to hell, I'll pick myself up, brush myself off and still become the next big name in the fashion world.

Chapter 18

Nicholas

My initial plan for this evening was to have dinner with Sophia, but she's got something going on that doesn't include me. I can't say I was surprised when she sent me that text message yesterday saying she was busy tonight. The woman could write a book on how to play hard to get. It should bother me enough that I give up on her and move on, but the challenge is too enticing. I want her and it's not just because I can't have her at the moment.

I've kissed hundreds of women in my life. Until the other day, I thought I possessed the ability to kiss a woman and walk away. I can't do that with Sophia. The kiss we shared only made me want her more. That hasn't changed.

What has changed is my method to try and distract myself from the non-stop thoughts of her that have overtaken my life. I managed to write a few thousand words early this morning but then my focus went to shit when I passed by the piano on my way to the kitchen.

I needed out of the apartment, so I fled. I walked through Central Park until I found myself on Fifth Avenue. A quick trip up the elevator of one of the most prestigious buildings on the block and I was in the office of an old friend.

Crew Benton, a guy I went to high school with, sought me out on social media a few months ago after he ran into Liam. We reignited our friendship and when I stopped by his office at Matiz Cosmetics earlier today, he invited me to join him tonight at a club he's investing in. He's hosting the soft launch and as much as I try to avoid the club scene unless I'm looking to hook-up, I agreed to tag along.

My motivation has everything to do with Sophia. I want a reprieve from the longing and I can't think of a better place than a club to make that a reality.

"Veil East," Crew says into his phone, his hand raking through his black hair. "I bought a club in Vegas, rebranded it as Veil West and you can fill in the blanks from there."

He rolls his eyes as he motions toward the bar. "I don't give a shit if you quote me directly or not. I want a feature piece on the front page of your website. You agreed to that so don't fuck with me now."

I laugh aloud as I listen to him talk to whoever the poor soul on the other end of that call is.

"Get me a scotch, Nick," he says as he moves the phone away from his mouth. "Order whatever you want. Drinks are on the house tonight."

"Fucking billionaire show off," I jest. "I'm ordering a bottle of whatever costs the most."

"Don't be a dick," he says that into the phone.

I walk through the large open space toward the bar. We arrived an hour before the doors are set to open and the club's employees are milling about, readying everything for the anticipated guests.

"Let me guess…" the curvy blonde behind the bar starts talking as I approach her. "Crew wants a scotch, right?"

"You know him too well." I laugh. "I'll take the same."

"Neat?"

"Sure." I nod. "Are you expecting a full house tonight?"

"We'll be at capacity within the hour." She slides two tumblers half full of scotch toward me. "I read *Burden's Proof*."

My brows lift in surprise. I shouldn't be shocked that she knows who I am. She's part of my target demographic. She's young and judging by the bare ring finger on her left hand, she's unattached. A solid part of my fan base is women just like her. "Did you like it?"

She leans over the bar until her tits are almost spilling out over the top of her black V-neck T-shirt. "I fucking loved it. I can't wait for *Action's Cause*. Can you give me a hint about what to expect?"

I'll never tire of this. The rush that comes from talking to someone about my work is addictive. "I can't. My publicist would kill me on the spot."

"Now, that would be a shame." She inches even closer, her tits straining against the thin fabric of her shirt. "My name is Penny, by the way."

I don't introduce myself because it's wasted effort. "Good to meet you, Penny. I need to get this drink to Crew before he comes looking for it."

"Come back when you need a refill, Nicholas."

I nod before I turn back toward where Crew is standing. If Penny isn't a sure thing, I don't know what is. Two weeks ago I would have been all over her by midnight and she would have been on her knees in a corner by the time her shift was done. Not tonight, though. Tonight, I'm keeping my dick where it belongs; in my jeans aching for a taste of Sophia.

***

I'm standing on a ledge on the upper concourse two hours later when I spot her in the club below. It should have been impossible to pick her out among the crowd of blending bodies, but the way she moves is unmistakable.

Sophia is here. She's in Veil East grinding against some hack in a two-piece gray suit that looks like it came off the rack at a fire sale. She, on the other hand, looks exquisite as always. Her dress is black and strapless. She's straightened her hair, so it falls loosely down her back. She looks edgy, sexy and when she turns in my direction, I can see that her lips are their signature deep red.

I grip the metal rail in front of me, my fingers stiff from anger. She plays hard-to-fucking-get with me, yet she's dancing like she's ready to screw the guy she's with.

She said she didn't have a boyfriend which means she's either a bigger liar than I thought, or he's a random hook-up.

"Penny can't keep her mouth shut about you, Nick." Crew slaps me from behind on the back. "You can use the executive office if you want to entertain her. I'm not against doing a favor for a friend."

"I'm not interested," I say over my shoulder. "Thanks for the offer though."

He steps in place beside me, a newly filled tumbler of scotch in his hand. "Are you seeing someone?"

"No," I answer quickly before I stumble back. "I was interested in someone, but that was a fucking waste of my time."

"What's going on?" He turns so he's facing me, his green eyes scanning my face. "You look like shit. What the hell happened in the past twenty minutes since I went downstairs?"

I draw in a deep breath of air. "I met a woman recently. I thought there was something between us but she's dry humping some idiot on the dance floor."

"Where?" He arches his neck out to look at the packed dance floor.

"It doesn't matter," I snap. "She blew me off with an excuse about having plans. Now I know."

"You know shit." He motions for one of the security guards dressed in a black suit to approach us. "Point her out and we'll get her up here. If you want her away from the guy she's dancing with, I can make that happen."

"Don't bother." I wave the burly security guard away. "What's the point?"

"The point is you want her."

I laugh loudly. "Not if she's out looking for a quick fuck."

"Who knew you had standards?" He chuckles before he takes a drink. "Tonight is invitation only. Point her out. Maybe I know her."

I don't know how the hell he thinks he can recognize anyone from our vantage point. It's a goddamn miracle that I spotted Sophia from where we are. "She's brunette, long hair, black strapless dress. She's in the middle of the floor practically crawling all over a brown-haired guy in a cheap suit."

He doesn't even bother to glance in the direction I'm pointing. Instead he looks right at me. "Does she have pale blue eyes, full red lips and an ass that should be illegal?"

I don't know whether to punch him or fall over from shock. "That's her."

He turns back to the security guard. "Go get, Sophia. Tell her I need to see her now."

Chapter 19

Sophia

I stare at him for a few seconds. Nicholas is standing in a private room in the VIP area of Veil East. He looks so fucking hot right now that I can barely control my desire to reach out and touch him, but I do. I stand in place, facing him and Crew.

Why is it that a guy can put on a pair of black pants and a white sweater and look like that? I seriously don't understand how any man can be as good-looking as Nicholas is.

"You two already know each other, so we'll skip the introductions." Crew approaches me with a chilled bottle of water in his hand. "Drink some of this, Sophia. You're dehydrated."

"I'm not," I protest but take the offered bottle. I unscrew the cap and swallow a large gulp. "Do you two know each other?"

"We went to high school together." Crew points at a booth. "Do you want to sit?"

"No." I drive the heel of my shoe into the carpet. "I want to know why you ordered me up here."

"How much have you had to drink?" Crew tugs his phone from his pocket. "Don't lie to me. I can call down and find out."

"No need, General Benton." I throw him a mock salute. "I had zero drinks tonight. I have to work on a dress when I get home so no alcohol for me."

"You dance like that when you're sober?"

Nicholas chuckles at Crew's obvious insult.

"What's wrong with the way I dance?" I shuffle my feet. "Did you call me up here to criticize my dance moves, Crew?"

"How do you two know each other?" Nicholas turns toward me. "Did you date each other?"

"No," I say too loudly. "No. There's no way. No."

"What the fuck, Sophia?" Crew throws his hands in the air. "You make it sound like a fate worse than death. I can tell you that I've never had a complaint from a woman."

"Never?" I concentrate on the smirk on his face. "I find that hard to believe."

He looks straight at Nicholas. "Sophia and I worked together about a year ago. We first met as she was walking out of one of our stores. I was on my way in and stopped her."

"You worked at Matiz?" Nicholas brows shoot up. "Haven't you been at Foster Enterprises longer than that?"

"I have." I let out a small sigh. "It complicated and we keep it quiet, but I did some modeling for Crew."

Crew opens the browser on his phone and pulls up a very familiar image from last year's fall lipstick campaign. "Do you recognize these lips, Nick?"

Nicholas takes the phone into his palm and studies the picture. It's a cropped photograph of my face. The only visible area is my lips, which are parted and painted a deep shade of red. My two front teeth are on display too.

I've never been recognized as the woman in the campaign ads and I haven't told anyone, other than Cadence, that it's me. It's not that I'm not proud of the work, but it was just a side job. Crew paid me well for a few hours of my time, including a lifetime supply of Matiz lipstick in any shade I want. I'm partial to red right now but come spring, I'll switch back to pale pink.

"I've seen this on a billboard in Times Square." Nicholas hands the phone back to Crew. "So you two know each other because of that?"

"We've become friendly since then." He holds us his hand to ward off any questions Nicholas might throw his way. "Platonic friends, Nick. I asked her out for a drink right after we met and she turned me down. I'm glad she did. I don't have a lot of female friends, but Sophia is an important one to me."

"Don't let this go to your head." I point my finger at Crew and give him the best stern expression I can muster. "Crew is my go-to when I need something. He's become one of my best friends in the city."

"Hear that?" Crew cups his hand over his left ear. "That's my heart melting because Sophia thinks I'm a stand-up guy."

"You're a jerk," I joke. "I'm trying to be nice, Crew."

"You're too nice." He taps the tip of my nose. "Here's an example, Sophia. You were way too fucking nice to whoever the hell that was you were dancing with just now."

Realization hits me like a speeding train. "Is that why I'm up here? You wanted to see me because I was dancing with Trey Hale?"

"Trey Hale?" Nicholas reaches for my bare bicep. "I read something online about the two of you from last year. I thought you tweeted that you didn't know him. Is that how you dance with men you don't know?"

My entire body shakes at his touch. "You're acting territorial, Nicholas. I'm allowed to dance with whoever the hell I want. We're not a couple. We're not anything right now."

"You're right." He releases my arm as he takes a step back. "We're nothing, Sophia. Enjoy your night."

With that he shakes Crew's hand, picks up a tumbler of scotch from the circular table near us and heads toward the elevator that leads to the dance floor.

***

"Do you think they're going to sleep together?" I stare down at the club. I've been watching Nicholas for the past ten minutes. Once he exited the elevator on the main floor, he made a beeline for the bar and the blonde bartender who seemed overly excited to see him.

"Nick and Penny?" Crew rests his hands on my shoulders. "He doesn't want her, Sophia."

"Are you blind?" I arch my neck back to look at his face. "Look at the way he's staring at her. Her tits are four times the size of mine."

"What do her tits have to do with this?" He digs his fingers into my shoulders. "You're way too fucking tense right now. You have to loosen up."

"I don't want him to fuck her," I say it under my breath. "I don't want that."

"He's blowing off some steam." He moves his fingers to the middle of my back. "You need to go down there and tell him what you want. You have to stop playing games with him."

I turn sharply leaving his hands hanging in mid-air. I reach for them both and squeeze them in mine. "I'm scared, Crew. He's different. He makes me want things."

"You make him want things." He bends his knees, so his face is aligned with mine. "He's a good guy, Sophia. He worked his ass off to get to where he is. Sure, he's been a man whore, but who the fuck wouldn't be when they're thrown into the life he has? Give him a chance."

"I told him I wanted him to chase me." I hang my head. "I made a huge deal about it. I liked that he wanted me, Crew. I liked that he was going out of his way for me."

He drops my hand and reaches to tilt my chin up, so I'm looking at him directly. "He saw you with Hale and it pissed him off. If he didn't care about you, he wouldn't have stuck around and waited for you to come up to talk to us. He wants you. If you feel the same way about him, stop fucking around."

"You think I should go down to the club and talk to him?"

"I think you should take him home tonight." He winks. "If I'm never going to have you, Nick is the second best choice for you."

"You know that you're like a brother to me, right?"

"Don't say shit like that when you look like that." His gaze travels down my body and back up. "I get that we didn't connect on that level, Sophia, but give Nick a chance. He's a better man than I am."

I look to the dance floor before I level my gaze back on his face. "I know I promised that I'd never say this to you again, but I have to."

"Don't." He drops my hand and takes a measured step back. "Sophia, don't."

"Adley is perfect for you," I say it even though he asked me not to. Adley is another of Crew's female friends. I've seen them together more than once and the chemistry that flows between the two of them is off the charts. "If you want me to give Nicholas a chance, I think you should agree to give Adley a chance."

"She's too good of a friend to fuck around with." His tone is firm. "I love Ad. I'll always love her but only as a friend. She doesn't see me as anything other than a pal and I sure as fuck don't see her any other way either."

"Time will tell." I brush a piece of lint off the skirt of my dress. "I'll drop the subject now. I promise."

"You better." He points at the waiting open elevator. "Get on that and go talk to Nick. You won't regret it."

"I hope not." I steal one last glance at Nicholas and the blonde bartender. "I think it's time I let him catch me. If I don't, I might lose my chance forever."

Chapter 20

Nicholas

I've been sitting at the bar waiting for Sophia for almost fifteen minutes. I have no doubt that she'll come looking for me. I saw the heated look on her face when she first saw me upstairs. She can tell me that she doesn't want me until her throat is raw, but I see it in her eyes. I watch the way her body reacts when I'm in the room.

I was angry earlier. I admit it, but there was more to it than that. I was fucking jealous. It's not an emotion I've had a lot of experience with, but I definitely felt it tonight when I watched her grinding on the guy on the dance floor.

When I heard her say Trey Hale's name, I lost it. I found that picture of the two of them on a street corner when I did my initial search for her online. Her tweets about the exchange they shared were playful and light. She commented that she didn't know him and that he was simply kissing her hand to thank her for giving him directions.

I haven't even fucked Sophia yet. If I get this torn up over seeing her with another man before I've touched her, I know there's no way in hell I'm going to be able to keep this thing between us casual.

"Nick?" Penny, the bartender, calls out my name. "Refill?"

I've downed two drinks already and although I don't feel the impact of either yet, I know from experience that I'm just a few sips away from falling over the edge into a light buzz. I have to stay grounded while I wait for Sophia. I don't want to lose my focus. There's shit I need to say. I'm tired of the goddamn games.

"No." My hand floats over my empty glass as she holds the open bottle perched at the ready. "Thanks, but I reached my limit."

"I have a break in fifteen." She taps the face of my watch with her index finger. "I'd love to show you the executive office. We could hang out in there. It's more private."

I glance up at the concourse of the VIP level. I can't make out anyone through the dim lights of the club. "I'm waiting for someone."

"You are?" Penny shoots me a look. "A woman?"

I curse silently. The frustrated expression on her face says it all. She thinks I was leading her on when in reality, I was just sitting next to the bar nursing a glass of scotch while she tried to guess the plot for *Action's Cause*. "It's a woman."

"That's one lucky bitch." Her gaze runs over me. "I have to say that she must be something special if you're turning me down."

Here I thought I had the biggest ego in the room. "She is."

I turn to face the private elevator that leads up to the VIP level. The doors fly open and I see Sophia when the man who was standing in front of her exits the lift. She pauses before she steps out, looks toward the bar and finally locks eyes with me.

***

I take Sophia's coat from her after I lock the door of my apartment. We didn't say more than a few words to each other at the club. She approached me, introduced herself to Penny and then asked if we could come here. I didn't argue with her.

We stopped at the coat check, three minutes later we slid into the backseat of one of the available taxis that had been waiting by the curb in front of the club. She stared out the window as we made our way here. I didn't push her to talk because I knew that the wheels were spinning in her head.

Sophia Reese needs to feel cherished. She wants to know that the men she fucks value her beyond the act. I get that now. Some asshole must have treated her like shit at some point in the past. I'm not him. I can prove that to her starting tonight.

"Do you want a glass of wine, Sophia?" I ask as she stands next to the piano. "You can play if you want. I won't stop you."

"I'll pass on the wine." She looks down at the keys. "And the piano. I'm not in the mood to play tonight."

I can't say I'm surprised. She's quieter than I've ever seen her before. "I'll skip the wine too."

She exhales roughly, her chest heaving with the motion. "Were you jealous when you saw me dancing with Trey?"

"Very." I stalk toward her, stopping just short of the piano bench that she's standing behind. "I didn't like it."

She holds my gaze. "I had no intention of going home with him. I want you to know that."

That thought hadn't crossed my mind until right this fucking minute. "Did he ask you to go home with him?"

"Twice. Both times I told him I only wanted to dance."

"Did you turn him down because of me?" My voice lowers. It's a loaded question, swollen with presumption but I want her to open up. I need her to be straight with me. We're wasting time edging around what we both feel. "Did you, Sophia?"

She leans back slightly. "I've never had a one night stand. Emotionally, I don't think I can do it. I feel things when I sleep with a man."

"Things?" I ask without thinking.

"I don't get all crazy obsessive or anything." She huffs out a nervous laugh. "I have to feel a connection before sex, and I like knowing there's a chance for a connection after sex too."

That's not how I view sex. I can sleep with a woman if I don't know her name and then never think about her again. I've done it dozens of times.

Her hands focus on the belt of her dress. She tugs on the end, knotting it more firmly in place. "I know it's probably different for you. I get that. I'm not saying that I need a relationship if we sleep together, but I don't want you to ignore me. If you think that's what will happen, I'd rather we make an agreement now to just be friends."

There's no way in hell I can just be friends with this woman. I'll always want more. "I don't want to be friends, Sophia. I want more."

"Sex?" Her jaw tenses. "You want to have sex with me?"

"Yes," I answer evenly. "I want to fuck you. I also want to take you out and spend time with you here and at your place. I want us to date."

Her fingers nervously yank harder on her belt, but her eyes stay trained on my face.

"You want it too." I sigh. "You feel the same things I do. You know this will be different. I'm not like the other men you've been with."

"You don't know them." Her arms cross. "I don't know the other women you've been with and I don't want to know."

"That suits me fine." I step closer. "We start tonight with a clean slate. Our pasts are just that. They're in the past. We agree to leave them there."

She pauses for a breath. "Agreed."

I take that as a cue and reach forward to touch her shoulders. She doesn't pull back. "You set the pace although I want to be clear that I've wanted to fuck you since you sat down next to me on the subway."

Her hands leap to the front of my sweater. "I know."

"It was the same for you," I state. It's not a question because we both know it's the truth.

"You're right." Her head tilts back as she looks up and into my eyes. "The chase is over. You caught me."

I close my eyes and move my lips to hers before I take her mouth in a deep, lush kiss.

Chapter 21

Sophia

A grin spreads across his face as he pulls back from what was a toe-curling kiss. "I have one thing I need to say, Sophia. I don't want you to fight me on this."

"We have to use condoms," I blurt out without thinking.

He cracks up. "I agree, but that's not what I was going to say. I didn't think using condoms was up for debate at this stage."

"Oh," I say with mild embarrassment. This is an important discussion. I don't want there to be any question about what I'm comfortable with. I take the pill but I know it's not foolproof and my five-year plan has no place in it for an unexpected newborn. "It's just that the last guy I dated wanted to go without and I walked out on him right before we fucked."

"You left him with a stiff dick?"

"Technically, he had a sheet covering that area." I circle my finger in front of his jeans. "He told me he didn't have condoms and when I went to get my purse to get one, he insisted that I skip the trip to the other room."

His eyebrow perks. "He sounds like an asshole."

"I never saw him again after that night." I smile. "I won't compromise on certain things and protection is one."

"Duly noted." He taps his forehead. "Condoms are mandatory. What else?"

I gaze up at the vaulted ceiling as if I'm in deep thought. This is what money affords a person in Manhattan. It's my second time here and I'm still noticing all the little touches that make this space spectacular. "I think that's it for tonight."

"Fair enough." He takes both my hands in his and rests them against the soft fabric that covers his chest. "I'll go back to what I was going to say originally."

I cringe. "I'm sorry. I took over the conversation."

"I'm glad you did." He lifts my hands and brings them to his lips for a gentle kiss. "I realize we haven't done anything beyond kissing; mind-blowing kissing."

"It *was* mind-blowing." I lean forward on my toes and give him a chaste kiss on the lips.

"If we're going to do this dating thing, I need something from you."

I eye him suspiciously. We barely know each other. We may have paved the way for a dating relationship, but we don't even know if we're compatible in bed. "What do you need?"

"I want us to be exclusive."

The muscles in his jaw tick as he waits for me to respond. I swallow, trying to think of what to say.

"Is that a problem?" He squares his shoulders as he squeezes my hands.

I clear my throat to afford me an extra second before I speak. "Why would you want to be exclusive with me when we haven't even slept together yet?"

He cocks his head to the side as he studies my face. "Fucking you is one part of the equation. I like hanging out with you. I want to cook for you and take you to the symphony. I'd like to wake up next to you on a lazy Saturday morning and then write while you work on sketching out a new design."

It's more than I've ever imagined. In my mind, I got as far as falling asleep in his arms in my bed after we'd made love. I didn't want to think it could reach beyond that, at least not at this stage. "We just met, Nicholas. We barely know each other."

"You're different than the other women I've known." He smiles down at me. "I know that I want to get to know you better without having to worry about Trey Hale getting in the way."

"You don't have to worry about him." I scrunch my nose. "I don't even like baseball."

"That's a start." He grips my waist and pulls me toward him. "If you want to go to a club, I'm always available."

"I'll keep that in mind." I tap my fingertips against his chest.

"Tell me what you want right now." He runs his nose along my jawbone, inhaling the scent of my skin. "I'll give you anything you want. I'll do anything you want."

I reach to cup his face in my hands, drawing his mouth closer to mine. I press my lips to his just as I whisper, "Take me to bed. Show me how much you want me."

***

His bedroom is just as imagined it would be in my mind's eye. The furniture is all crafted from a rich dark wood including the massive headboard. There's a small chest of drawers near the window and a larger, sleek cabinet that stands next to the door that leads into the room.

The bed linens are masculine. The duvet is dark gray, the pillow cases and sheets a stark black. The only light in the room is escaping from the adjoined washroom which, from this vantage point, contains a claw foot tub and a quartz countertop atop a vanity that houses two sinks.

It's a space any bachelor would crave, complete with a fireplace and a flat screen television hung above it.

There's an open laptop on a desk near the window. Several notepads sit nearby stacked in an uneven pile. Next to them is a trio of pens, all of them are identical. They're silver, just like the one he pulled from his bag on the subway.

"Is that where the magic happens?"

He turns at the sound of my voice. "The magic? Is that what we're calling it now? I prefer to call it *fucking* or, depending on my mood, *making love*. I guess it could be considered magic, so the answer to your question is yes. The bed is where the magic is going to happen. Don't consider yourself just an assistant though. I expect full participation in all tricks."

I can't help but laugh. "I was asking about the desk, not the bed. Do you write at that desk?"

He schools his expression to look more serious than he is. The slight smile on his lips hints at his amusement. "Any magic that happens in this room is on that bed. I sleep there, I write there and tonight, I'm going to make you come there."

He pulls his sweater over his head to reveal a toned stomach and chest. It's obvious the man works out. His abs are evidence of his commitment to himself.

"Your turn, Sophia." He gestures at my dress.

"You have an unfair advantage." I slip off both of my heels. "I'm wearing a lot less clothing than you are."

"You're not." He inches closer a few steps before he toes out of his shoes and removes his black socks. "Drop the dress and I'll lose the pants."

"Is that an offer or an order?" I playfully pull on the sash of my dress.

He unbuckles the black belt he's wearing before he slides it free from his pants. "Call it what you will. I want to see your body."

I want to see his too. My eyes have been riveted to the light trail of dark hair that begins just below his belly button and disappears beneath the waistband of his pants. "Show me your body first."

"Get on the bed."

"What?" I look at the bed before I turn my attention back to him.

He stalks toward me, his hands reaching for my forearms. "I want you on the bed, Sophia."

"Don't you want me to strip?" I ask nervously. "You said you want to see my body."

He pushes me back, each step inches us both closer to his bed. "I need to touch you more than I want to see."

I let him guide me to the bed and when he pushes me back tenderly, I bend my knees and sit on the edge.

"On your back." He's standing in front of me now, the front of his pants hovering next to my face. "I want you on your back. We'll take this slowly."

I'm not sure that's what I want anymore. He's two seconds away from being completely nude and I've wondered, for days, what his cock looks like. I've imagined it based on what I've felt when he's pressed himself against me. I know he's thick. I can tell that he's going to be larger than any of the men I've been with before.

I slide my ass back to the middle of the bed before I sprawl out on my back. I cross my legs at the ankles, trying desperately to keep my skirt in place.

He crawls over me until his hands are splayed on the duvet on either side of my head. His legs bracket me. I can feel his swollen cock rubbing against my stomach through the fabric of my dress and his pants.

"Will you kiss me now?" I ask breathlessly. I need him to touch me. I want that.

He does. He lowers his face until his lips catch mine in a kiss. He takes it slowly, teasing me with his tongue. His licks are deep and leisurely. He moans when I try and bite his bottom lip.

"I need to make you come." He whispers those heated words as he breaks the kiss.

"Now?" I practically pant. I can feel my arousal pooling between my legs. I know when he reaches down to touch my panties, they'll be sopping wet.

He moves his lips lower until they're grazing over the soft skin of my neck.

"Relax, Sophia." His breath tickles my chest. "I promise this won't hurt a bit."

Chapter 22

Nicholas

I have no fucking idea why I'm not inside of her yet. As soon as she whispered that she wanted me to take her to bed, I could feel a drop of pre-cum already sitting on the crown of my dick. I'm still hard as a rod of steel, but this isn't going to be about me. I want tonight to be about Sophia.

Before I seal my mouth over hers, I look down at her. She's prone on her back underneath me. I've felt her legs fidgeting since I straddled her. She may be trying to convey the demeanor of a woman who has fucked countless other men, but her body says otherwise.

She moans softly into our kiss, her hands leaping to the back of my head. I lick deep into her mouth, coaxing her tongue to touch mine. I want her to enjoy this as much as she would if I was balls deep inside her beautiful body.

I pull back so I can see what my touch does to her. I have to capture that second when she explodes around my hand and that starts now.

I roll off of her and press my body against her side. Her chest is heaving; short, quick bursts of breath that reveal her need.

"Are you going to undress me?" She turns her head to look at me. "If you are, be careful because this fabric rips easily."

I chuckle. "I'll keep that in mind. For tonight, I think I'd rather see you come undone with your clothes on."

She frowns. "You're going to fuck me while I'm dressed?"

I slide my fingertip along her collarbone before I dip it down to the front of her dress. It's strapless and it's obvious that she didn't bother with a bra. Her nipples are pressing against the fabric, straining for attention. I circle the right one, through the fabric of her dress, my finger tracing a circular path around the hard nub. "Your tits are a perfect size."

"I've always thought so." She smiles at me. "I'm glad you like smaller breasts."

I've never had a preference until now. Her body is everything any man could want and that's not just because of her sensual curves.

Trey Hale might have been the one grinding against her ass in the club, but there were dozens of eyes on her. When she exited the elevator, several men turned to watch her walk by. She commands attention, even if she's completely oblivious to it.

Reaching down I sweep my hand over her smooth thigh. She doesn't resist. Her desire to get off takes over and her legs part slightly.

"You're wet, aren't you?" I press my lips to the skin of her neck. "You've been wet since you saw me at the club."

She nods silently.

"Did you want me then, Sophia? Did you want me to reach under your dress and touch you like this?" I inch my hand up until my fingers rest on the lace of her panties.

"I did." The words are so low I can barely make them out.

I pull her panties aside and glide my fingers over the smooth flesh. "Spread your legs."

She closes her eyes and shifts her legs, spreading them wide, slinging one over my thigh.

"Good." I bite back a moan of my own. She's so fucking wet that I could slide my cock right in without any resistance. I want that. I want to feel her heat wrapped around me. Hell, now I get where that asshole she talked about was coming from. Who in their right mind would want a barrier between her cunt and their cock?

I kiss her again. My tongue probes her mouth as I slide a finger, and then two, inside her slick wetness.

"You'll come for me like this."

"Yes," she whispers into my lips.

I flick her swollen clit with my thumb, strumming an uneven beat that she tries to mimic with the roll of her hips. She's chasing it now. She wants it as badly as I do.

I slow and she growls out a tight, "No."

"If you come like this, I won't fuck you tonight." I nip the lobe of her ear with my teeth. "It's your choice. Take it like this or take me."

She stills in place, but I don't stop. I continue my tender exploration of her body, picking up the pace of my thumb.

"I want to fuck," she mewls.

"You control it all," I say as I slide my fingers inside of her and increase the tempo. I fuck her pussy hard, my hand moving at a fevered pace.

"Oh God." Her voice is edgy and deep. "I'm close."

I can tell. Her wetness coats my fingers and I can feel it dripping down her, covering her ass. "Your pussy is on fire. It's so soft, so wet, Sophia."

She gasps but it's not from my words, it's the impending approach of an orgasm that is going to tear her apart.

"Tell me to stop if you want my cock," I growl in her ear.

She's too far gone. Her hand bolts down to mine, holding it in place as she rides my fingers to a scream-inducing orgasm that almost makes me blow my load.

***

I held Sophia as she came down from the high of her release. I should have stripped, ripped her panties from her body and fucked her until I came myself, but I didn't. I pulled her into my chest and listened to her breathing. It stalled two times before it finally calmed and then settled into the ragged breaths of sleep.

I unwound myself from her carefully, watching her face for any signs that I was disturbing her but she slept through it all. Once I was free of the bed, I shed my pants and boxers, slipped on a pair of black sweatpants and covered her with a soft blanket.

I'm in my kitchen now, a mug of hot coffee by my side as I outline the still unnamed book that will follow up the release of *Action's Cause*.

My hands hover above my keyboard when I hear the faintest sound coming from the hall. I look up.

Fuck.

Sophia is there, her hip leaning against the wall. She's not wearing the dress anymore. Now, she's wrapped in one of my sweaters, a gray one with oversized buttons down the front, although she's only fastened one in the middle, shielding her tits from my view. Her black lace panties are on full display though.

Her legs are toned and long considering her height. Her hips are wide. She's a vision and I have no idea what the fuck to say to her.

She clears her throat before she drags her hand over her forehead, chasing away a few strands of hair. "I fell asleep."

"You did." I pat the stool next to me. "Come and sit."

"Can I play?" She gestures toward the piano. "I have an urge to play."

I can't deny her even though I want nothing more than to bend her over the counter and fuck her from behind. "You know how it works. You'll pay to play."

Her tongue darts out to coat her bottom lip. "I'm counting on that."

I don't ignore my swollen cock. Instead, I reach down and squeeze the tip through my sweatpants. "Play, Sophia."

She pads quickly across the room before she sits down on the bench. A small, "Oh," escapes her. It's an audible sign of the sensation of her ass hitting the cool leather of the bench. She places her hands on the keys as she turns to me. "Do you have a request?"

My knowledge of classical music is limited to what I've heard when I'm gone to the symphony. I don't listen to it. My phone is filled with music produced and recorded this year. I don't want to disappoint her so I say the only thing I can think of. "Surprise me."

"I can do that." She slides another piece of hair behind her ear. "This is one of my favorites. Sing along if you know the words."

I laugh loudly. This playful side of her is what I crave. I want this, all of it; her semi-nude at my piano with a glow on her face that I gave to her.

I get up and cross the room until I'm sitting in the black leather arm chair next to the piano. I lean back and close my eyes as she begins to play.

Chapter 23

Sophia

I played a piece by Chopin. It sprang from my fingers once I pressed the first key. I watched Nicholas intently as I finished. His eyes were closed. His head was resting against the back of the chair with his hands folded loosely in his lap.

"That was beautiful," he says without opening his eyes. "Come and sit on my lap."

I don't hesitate. I move quickly across the cold hardwood floors until I settle in his lap, my back resting against the arm of the chair. I can feel his erection. He wants me still, even after I selfishly took from him in the bedroom.

"I chose myself instead of you," I whisper as I rest my lips against his forehead. "I should have told you to stop so you could fuck me."

His eyes open lazily. "I want you to take, Sophia. I want you to use my body. I loved what we did earlier."

"You did?" I tug on the bottom of the sweater, but it's useless. My panties are visible. They're sheer lace so he can see my pussy if he glances down.

He does right then. "I licked my fingers clean. You taste amazing."

I blush. I'm grateful that the room is dark enough that he can't tell. "Really?"

"I was tempted to go down on your right there, but you fell asleep." He rests his chin on my bended knee. "Maybe you should slide those off and sit on my face now."

I want that. I know that he'll be as good with his mouth as he is with his fingers. "Is that what playing the piano will cost me?"

"Not tonight." He shakes his head as his hand snakes up my calf. "You're going to strip and fuck me in this chair."

My pussy clenches at the command. There's no debate. I won't argue with him. I want it as much as he does.

"Do you have a condom?" I ask as I stand to take my panties off.

He leans forward to press his lips to my stomach. "I'll go get one. Don't move a muscle."

I step out of the way so he can rush past me to the bedroom. I consider following him, but he told me to stand still so that's exactly what I do. My eyes scan the area around me. I've been oblivious to everything in this room but the piano. My gaze finally settles on a trio of picture frames on a table near the chair we were just sitting in.

Nicholas is in all three of the photographs. One is of him, a woman and two other men. All of them resemble him, so it's easy to assume they're his siblings. The second is of him with an older woman, who shares the same blue eyes as him. That must be his mom.

It's the third picture that steals my attention. He's much younger in it. The angles of his jaw are softer, his hair a bushy mess. He's standing next to a girl who looks to be close to his age. She's wearing denim cut-offs and a billowy white blouse. There's no family resemblance between them. It's not surprising since their body language speaks of lovers and not of kin.

"You follow directions very well." His breath rushes over my cheek as his arms circle me.

I jump, startled that I was so lost in thought that I didn't hear him come back into the room. "You told me to stand still."

"That I did." He uses his index finger and thumb to open the only fastened button on the sweater.

I moan when I feel his hand on my breast. "You want to do this here? We could go to your bed."

"You're going to ride me, Sophia." He slides the sweater from my shoulders. "Take off your panties."

I do, my eyes still trained on the picture of Nicholas and a girl who was important enough to him to warrant a coveted spot next to his family. It shouldn't matter now. He's obviously moved past her since the picture was taken at least ten years ago. I still have a memento, or two from my first love tucked away in the corner of my desk drawer.

He spins me around so quickly that I have to brace my hands on his biceps for balance. My eyes fall to his nude body and already sheathed thick cock.

"Wow," I say loudly. "That's…it's wow."

"If wow means you like it, I'll take that." He nudges his nose against my neck." I'll sit down. I want you to stand here and touch yourself until you're ready."

I've never done that in front of a man before. When I'm at home, I always pull the sheet up around my breasts before I masturbate. "I think I'm ready. If I'm not, you can touch me."

He sits in the chair, his ass moving until he's positioned exactly where he wants to be. "Show me how you get yourself off."

I fidget on my feet, suddenly aware that my entire body is visible to him. "I can't."

"You can." He reaches for my hand. "Your pussy is so soft. Touch it for me."

I close my eyes and let him guide my fingers to my core. I'm already wet. I was the entire time I was playing the piano because I knew that there was a price to pay. I wanted it to be his cock in my mouth but the thought of riding him to orgasm is even better.

I relax as he pushes my fingers between my folds. His hand moves with mine until his drops away. I hesitate before I continue, circling my clit with the tip of my index finger.

"That's so fucking beautiful."

I open my eyes to see him in front of me, his cock in his hand. "I'm ready."

"Get yourself close." His eyes are hooded. "I want you on me when you're almost ready to come."

I move my fingers faster, hunting for my release. "It won't take long. You're incredible to look at."

"You like this?" He palms his sheathed cock. "You're going to ride it, Sophia. You're going to show me how badly you've wanted to fuck me."

So bad. I've wanted it so much.

I moan as I feel the fevered pitch of an orgasm nearing.

"Come." He holds out his hand to me, guiding me closer to the chair. "Slide onto me. Slowly."

It has to be slow. He's wide and I'm anxious when I feel the crown touch my opening. I brace myself with one hand behind him on the back of the chair, as I circle his cock with my other hand.

"Slide down, Sophia." His breath comes out in a ragged gasp. "Fuck, this is hot."

It is. I look down at where we're joined. He's barely inside me yet I feel completely full. I move again, taking more and it stretches. It's not to the point of pain, but it's edging there, a delicious mixture of pleasure mixed with fullness.

His hands jump to my hips to control my movement. "Christ, you're going to fucking kill me with this."

I moan when he slams my hips down, burying himself in me. The sensation is almost too much and I grip the chair with both hands, my fingernails digging into the leather.

"Fuck me," he growls against my neck. "Take it, Sophia. Use my cock."

I do. I move, slow at first and once I adjust, I arch my back and slide back and forth. He lets me set the pace until his body takes over and he rams up and into me in a series of steady, deep jabs.

"Like that." His words are deep and husky. "Just like that."

I ride him just like that until I come apart in his arms and then he takes what he wants, fucking me hard until I feel the warmth of his release when he calls out my name.

Chapter 24

Nicholas

"I assume last night went well." Crew eyes me when I walk up to where he's sitting at the café he told me to meet him at. "You look satisfied, Nick."

He knows Sophia so there's no fucking way I'm going into details about what happened at my place last night even though it was incredible. She fucked me in the chair next to the piano before she slid off me and covered herself with the sweater. Her beautiful pussy was still on display so after I tied off the condom and tossed it into the wastebasket, I threw her in the chair, got on my knees and ate my way to pure joy. I licked that sweet pussy while she squirmed beneath my tongue. She came twice before she pushed me away and told me she had to go.

I didn't take her home even though I wanted to follow behind her. I called for a car from the service I sometimes use and she left in the same dress she arrived in although I found her panties this morning next to the piano.

"That's none of your fucking business."

He flashes a big smile. "I'll take that as a yes. I won't pry but dammit, Nick, I've got to say I'm envious."

I'm not surprised. Sophia was incredible. I'm already aching for another taste.

"Why the meeting?" I look at the counter and the long line of people gathered near it. "You could have picked a place that isn't so popular. I'm not standing in that line to get a coffee."

"You don't have to." He looks over his shoulder at a tall brunette wearing one of the signature yellow aprons of the small chain of cafes in Manhattan. She's cleaning plastic trays although her gaze is glued to the back of Crew's head "Chelsey, my friend needs a coffee. Can you bring him one of the fancy ones you brought me?"

She walks toward us, her hands busily adjusting her ponytail. "Sure thing, Crew. Do you want anything else?"

"You at my office Monday afternoon at four," he says with a sly wink. "Can you make that happen?"

She almost vibrates from excitement. "Are you serious? I can be there. I will be there."

"I'll give you the address before I take off."

She catches my gaze before she looks back at Crew. "I know where it is. I'll get right on that drink for your friend."

"You're the best." He shoots me a look before he turns back to her. "We both appreciate it."

I wait until she's out of earshot before I say a thing. "How old is she, Crew?"

"She's a freshman at NYU." He laughs. "You didn't think I was inviting her to my office so I could screw her, did you?"

As uncomfortable as the thought was, it did cross my mind. I would have pegged her for a high school kid. "Why did you invite her to your office?"

"I ran into her agent a few days ago. He had some test shots of her he wanted me to see." He looks to where Chelsey is standing behind the counter, her focus intent on the task at hand. "Her eyes are killer; smoky blue and wide. She's perfect for the summer campaign we're about to shoot for Matiz. It's a new eyeliner and shadow."

"You're going to give her a job for getting me a coffee?"

"Fuck, no." He leans back and crosses his arms over his chest. "Her parents own this place. They've been pushing free coffee my way for months."

***

An hour later, I'm back on my own with a newfound appreciation for Crew's business acumen. The man has a hand in the running of at least six different businesses and he's looking to expand his portfolio. His new venture involves a friend of his who designs shoes and handbags. He sees it as having guaranteed investment potential and he wants me, or more accurately, my money on board. I hesitated when he asked because the thought struck me that if I'm going to invest anything in the world of fashion; I want my money backing Sophia.

What does my favorite fashion designer like to do on Saturdays?

I type that out and send it to Sophia as I near the corner of Broadway and Columbus. I'm on the Upper West Side to stop by my folks' place to surprise them. I don't call ahead anymore because that always leads to a dinner invitation that turns into an inevitable conversation about all the mistakes I made when I was a kid.

My current success may impress a lot of people but I don't count my parents as two of them. My dad expected me to follow in his footsteps and earn a badge. I never wanted to be a member of the NYPD. It's not in my blood the way it is for him and Sebastian.

I needed to write and through the lean years, my mom slipped me money whenever she could, but the onus was on me to make ends meet. I did. After college, I moved into a shitty walk up that already housed six other guys. I slept on the floor in a sleeping bag for a week before I emptied my bank account to buy a folding cot. I made it work because I had to.

When it came time for Liam to face the biggest decision of his life, he took another career route altogether. His choice was easier for my folks to accept because he healed those left behind by the senseless crime in this city.

My phone vibrates in my hand as I wait for the light to cross.

I eat donuts and design maternity clothes. What about you?

I step off the curb and start typing, following the crowd as they cross the street.

Going to visit my folks.

I wait for a response and stop on the sidewalk once I see it.

They live in the city?

Uptown. I type back before I press send.

There's a pause before I see her typing.

I'm heading uptown in two hours. It's half price today at my favorite fabric place.

I should invite myself along, but I've got some place I need to be after this.

Do you wanna come with? I could use you as a model.

I stare down at the screen, clenching my phone in my fingers so hard it's liable to bend in half.

Fuck.

Can't. I've got plans.

I make it all the way to the lobby of my parents' building before I finally hear the chime on my phone signaling a new message.

No problem. Have a good day, Nicholas.

You too. I press send even though I want to tell her what I'm doing. I can't yet. It's too much. If she knows what's lurking in my past, I may never see her again.

Chapter 25

Sophia

"Why are you sitting at home on a Saturday night?" Cadence pushes my feet aside so she can sit next to me on the couch. The aroma of the popcorn she just made fills the room. "I thought you'd be out on a date with the great American novelist."

I thought I would be too. I wasn't all that surprised when Nicholas turned down my invitation to meet me at the fabric store. I don't know another soul who would want to spend an entire Saturday afternoon checking out hundreds of rolls of discounted fabric. I totally get that, but I was curious when he said he had other plans and then didn't elaborate.

We had that awkward conversation about only dating each other a few days ago, but we haven't touched on it since. If he's changed his mind, I'm not going to pout. I just want to know where I stand with him.

"Are you saying you'd rather be at home alone?" I push my bare foot into the side of her jean covered thigh. "I know Tyler pulls a shift every Saturday night because he can't stand the thought of anyone but him being at Nova's helm on the busiest night of the week."

"That's word-for-word what I said to you when he started working weekends." She arches a brow. "You know how he is. He owns the place. If something goes wrong, it's all on him."

"I get it." I do. I'm the same way with my designs. I tweak them incessantly until I think they look perfect. It's not because I have the pressure on me that Tyler does. No one knows about my work yet, but when I do get discovered, I want to be certain that it's smooth sailing from that day forward.

She stretches her arm along the back of the sofa as she pops a piece of popcorn in her mouth. "I want to talk about Nicholas. Have you seen him again?"

All of him, as a matter of fact.

"I saw him last night," I say as I push the remote to pause the program we've been watching. It's an episode of our favorite police procedural. We started the habit of watching it together when we were roommates and now I always wait for Cadence to come over before I order a new episode on Netflix.

"I thought you went to that club opening last night." Her eyes volley between the frozen image of a police officer with a gun in his hand on TV and my face.

I sigh heavily. "He was there."

"Nicholas was there?"

I take a minute to reply. I could easily get her off the topic of what happened between Nicholas and me if I bring up Trey Hale. It was a brief encounter that isn't worth mentioning though. She's my best friend, so I shouldn't hide the truth from her even if it sends her into a romantic frenzy. "He was. We left together."

The large bowl of popcorn in her lap almost tumbles over as she turns to look at my face. "Sophia, what the hell? Why didn't you tell me this the second I walked in?"

"Because I knew you'd act like this." I scoot my ass across the couch so I can sit upright. "It was just sex, Cadence. I had sex with him at his place."

"It's not just sex." She moves to put the bowl of popcorn on the coffee table. "It's sex with Nicholas Wolf."

"What is that supposed to mean?" I reach for a handful of popcorn and toss a piece in the air before I catch it in my mouth. "He's just a man, Cadence. He's a man who happens to write books."

"He's not just a man," she mimics my tone but adds a noticeable dash of sarcasm. "He's one of the hottest men on the planet and you slept with him."

"He is hot," I acquiesce as I toss a piece of popcorn too high and it coasts over my head before hitting the hardwood floor behind me. "We had fun and then today I invited him to tag along with me to buy some fabric and he said he had other plans."

"I would have ditched on that too." She laughs. "I've gone fabric shopping with you, Soph. It's not a fun time."

My mouth curves into an unwanted, but uncontrollable, smile. "I know. It's just that he was uptown and I was headed uptown and I assumed he'd want to see me after last night."

"You thought he'd want to follow you around a cramped fabric store for hours because the sex was that good?"

"When you put it like that, I see your point." I throw the last piece of popcorn in my hand at her. She watches it fly past her nose before it lands on one of the red throw pillows she left here when she moved.

"Let him decompress, Soph." She reaches to grab the remote from where I put it on the table. "Give him a couple of days and he'll be all over you again."

I know she's right. We had too good a time last night for him to brush me off. I should be thinking about our next date with butterflies in my stomach but the only thing rooted in my gut is a niggling feeling that the girl in the photograph I saw last night, may not be completely out of the picture.

***

"Your website is a work of shit," Joe, the tech guy, that Nicholas connected me with laughs. It's one of those deep chuckles that lure the attention of every person around us. That might be fine if we weren't sitting in the staff lunchroom of Foster Enterprises headquarters.

Several of my co-workers turn to look at us. I toss them a polite smile hoping they'll get back to their microwave warmed lunches.

"Nicholas told me it was bad, but Sophie, this is the worst."

"It's Sophia," I say as I take a bite of the apple I brought with me today. I knew I'd be having this meeting at lunch so packing something more substantial didn't make any sense.

"Sure, Sophia." He gazes over the top of his laptop screen at me. "When Nick called me yesterday to ask me to do this, he didn't tell me you were so blazing."

Does that mean hot?

It doesn't matter. What does matter, even though it shouldn't, is that he heard from Nicholas yesterday and I haven't heard a peep out of him since our text exchange on Saturday afternoon.

Joe's a guy, so I'm tempted to ask him what the current protocol is for texting a woman after you've fucked her brains out. I resist that urge and instead focus on the matter at hand.

"I don't think it's all that bad." I lean back on the plastic chair I'm sitting on. "I do respect your opinion so tell me what I can do to improve it."

"Start from scratch." He accompanies that comment with an actual scratch to his overgrown dark beard. "The mess you've got going on now is unfixable."

I glance around the room before I lean in closer. "My finances are tight right now. Can you do anything for say, five hundred dollars?"

"Beautiful and cheap?" His hand leaps to his chest. "You're a woman after my own heart."

"I'm not cheap," I correct him in a hushed tone. "Most of my resources go into my business. I design clothes."

"Duh." He points to the screen of his laptop with both of his index fingers. "I'm looking at your website right now. I see what you've got going on."

"Can you spice it up for five hundred?" I finish the last bite of the apple. "I'd appreciate anything you can do that would make it look edgier."

He snaps the cover of his computer closed before he rests his elbows on the circular white table we're sitting next to. "You know that Nick is footing the bill for this, right? He wants your input on everything design related, but he's covering the cost of a complete overhaul of your site."

"No." I shake my head as I drop the apple core in my empty coffee cup. "I don't want him to do that."

"It's already done." He thumps his front shirt pocket and the top of the small weathered billfold that is visible. "He paid me yesterday and the cash is tucked away in my account. Between you and me, it's the only money in my account right now."

"Why would he pay for it?" I ask myself as much as him.

He looks over at the table next to us where three women are sitting. "Isn't it obvious? Men will do anything for a woman they want."

That might be true, but I'm not for sale. Before this day is over, Nicholas Wolf is going to understand that I take care of myself.

Chapter 26

Nicholas

My gaze runs over Sophia as soon as she enters through the revolving door. She sent me a text an hour ago asking me to meet her in the lobby of a luxury hotel that borders Central Park. I asked what it was about, but the only response she sent was an address to this place.

I'm not familiar with it. I don't frequent hotels in the city since I established an office space that is separate from my apartment. I admit that I once kept a room at a cut-rate hotel in Hell's Kitchen that I used exclusively as a place to fuck. I outgrew it quickly though since it left me feeling as cheap and used as I'm sure the women I took there felt.

"Nicholas." She nods as she approaches, the buttons on her white coat flying open as she skims her fingers over them to reveal a dark navy skirt and light blue top underneath. She slides the coat off with little effort before draping it over her left forearm. "There's a bar across the lobby. It's easier to talk in there."

To talk.

The words and her tone are both ominous. The look in her eye is the same.

I didn't like saying no to her two days ago when she texted me asking if I wanted to go to a fabric shop with her. Her demeanor at this moment doesn't reflect that of a woman who was turned down in the middle of a weekend afternoon. There's more brewing below the surface. Something's pissed Sophia off and I'm standing in the middle of that shit storm.

"Lead the way." I raise my hand in the air and complete the movement with a slight bow. "You're running this show."

She turns on her heel and starts to cross the lobby, only stopping briefly to wave at a man dressed in an impeccable black three-piece suit. Envy rolls through me. He's my age, or younger and apparently, his mere presence deserves a cheerful, open smile from the woman I fucked not even three days ago.

"Who was that?" I ask as I fall into step beside her.

She doesn't break her pace as we near the entrance to the hotel bar. "A friend."

I don't press for more because I'm the one following her into a bar for a drink and the three-piece suit schmuck is still standing in the lobby with his mouth hanging open at the sight of her voluptuous ass in the too-tight skirt. "What are we going to talk about?"

"I called earlier," she ignores my question as she stops to talk to a woman with jaw length blonde hair standing near the entrance to the bar. "I'm Sophia Reese."

"You're Mr. Foster's assistant." The woman looks right past me. "Is Gabriel joining you? He hasn't been here in months."

"He considers himself a silent partner in the hotel." Sophia peers into the dimly lit bar. "I can tell him you said hello when I see him tomorrow."

"Would you?" She adjusts the nametag pinned to the front of her simple black dress. "It's Hannah. We met the night the hotel opened. I'll never forget how kind he was to the entire staff."

Sophia smiles a little. "He's a good man. I'm lucky that I get to work so closely with him."

Hannah gives her what looks like a knowing wink. It has to be an inside joke because I'm still standing right behind Sophia in silence since she didn't bother to introduce me.

"Your table is in the back." Hannah reaches for Sophia's coat. "I'll put this behind the bar. Come find me when you're ready to leave."

Sophia nods and then finally turns back to look at me. "This way."

I trail behind her like a dog looking for scraps as she darts past the people who've gathered in the bar. It's a small space and judging by the wall of bodies we have to maneuver around, it's popular too.

"He's already here," Sophia calls back over her shoulder.

"Who?" I yell over the hum of the voices that are all blending together in an uneven buzz.

She cocks her head at me and laughs like I should know what the ever loving fuck she's talking about. I feel like a lamb being led to its slaughter.

Resigned, I follow her to wherever the hell she's taking me knowing that at the end of this journey there's some nameless guy waiting for us. I thought it was going to be just the two of us sharing a drink but apparently Sophia's into threesomes. I'm not if they involve another dick.

I glance over her shoulder and that's when I spot him. He's standing near a table talking to a tall, attractive brunette. He may have shaved off his beard and traded his signature ripped T-shirt and jeans for a suit, but it's clear that Joe, my tech guy, is the man Sophia brought me here to see.

***

"Nick, my man, how the hell is it hanging?"

Sophia cringes at Joe's words. "Don't ask that. You should never ask that question to anyone again."

"Why the fuck not?" Joe looks down his nose at Sophia.

She gives him some serious side eye before she turns to look at him directly. "You're not a fourteen-year-old kid, Joe. You're the head of the tech department at Foster Enterprises now. Start acting like it."

"He's what?" I ask, my eyes darting from Sophia's face to Joe's almost unrecognizable one. "Since when do you work at Foster?"

"Since this beauty landed me a full-time job." He elbows Sophia. "I get a corner office, benefits and control over their entire tech department. I'm going to be making six figures a year, Nick. Can you fucking believe it?"

I can't. I seriously can't. "How did this happen?"

Sophia cants her head toward his hands. "Give it to him now, Joe."

"Do I have to?" He stiffens. "I thought you might reconsider."

"If you don't," Sophia begins as she takes a small step toward Joe. "If you don't give it to Nicholas now, I can call Mr. Foster and tell him I made a mistake."

"Jesus, you drive a hard bargain, Sophie."

"Sophia," she corrects him with a smile.

"I know." He studies her, the look in his eye raising my pulse. He's attracted to her. I can't blame him for that. "It's my nickname for you."

"Drop it." Her tone is neutral. "We had an agreement, Joe. If you back out, I'll make sure you never step foot in your new office again."

"I fucking believe you." His hand disappears into the left pocket of his jacket. When it reappears, there's a wad of bills in his palm. He pushes it at me. "Here's the money you gave me to fix her website. Our deal is off, Nick."

I look down at the cash. "I paid you to help Sophia. Nothing's changed."

Sophia snatches the money from Joe before she tucks it in the pocket of my coat. "Everything's changed, Nicholas."

Chapter 27

Sophia

Nicholas sits in the corner of our booth with an untouched tumbler of scotch on the table in front of him. He hasn't said a word since I pushed the money he gave Joe into his pocket. I brought him here to show him that I'm one woman who is more than capable of finding her own way to pay for a website overhaul.

"After I met Joe yesterday, I realized that Foster Enterprises has been looking for someone to helm the tech department for over a month. Mr. Foster and his brother haven't been impressed with any of the applicants, so I asked Joe to clean himself up and come in for an interview."

It's the truth, mostly the truth.

I did think of Joe when I saw yet another interoffice memo about all the available job openings at Foster. It was waiting for me in my inbox when I got back to my desk after lunch. Since the listing at the top was for the tech department, I immediately thought of Joe. I sent him a brief text message asking if he would be interested in a full-time gig with great benefits and an even better salary.

He texted me back almost immediately saying he might be since the money Nicholas gave him was all he had to his name. It was the second time that he'd mentioned his cash flow problem to me so I told him I'd arrange an interview but I expected a favor if he landed the job.

Knowing exactly what I was after, he agreed. Three hours later he arrived at my desk, clean-shaven and dressed in a suit. Mr. Foster gave him the job on the spot and before Joe left the building, we had an agreement in place that he'd build me a new website, and maintain it on a monthly basis, at no charge.

"I take it the price for helping him land the job involves him doing side work for your design business for free?" Nicholas finally picks up his drink.

I nod as I sip on the glass of red wine I ordered. "It's not that I didn't appreciate you hiring him to help me. I did, but it felt like too much too soon."

He puts the tumbler down without bringing it to his lips. "I wanted to help you. You have so much potential, Sophia. I saw it as a sound investment in you. I have no doubt you're going to rule the New York fashion scene one day."

I smile brightly at the compliment. "It's not an actual investment if there's no legal contract drawn up. You were doing me a favor. It's too generous a favor for anyone to do for a person they just met."

I can tell by his reaction that my words sting. "Should we get a legal contract drawn up? I have some funds I'm looking to invest. I'd gladly buy some shares in your company."

It's not technically an actual company. I took the preliminary steps to get everything set up a few months ago when I thought I might be able to sell some pieces in a store owned by the husband of a woman Cadence worked with. That never panned out, so I used the money I'd set aside for lawyer fees to buy more supplies.

"I'm not at the point where I'm looking for investors yet," I say as I make a mental note to check in with Zoe Beck, a friend of a friend who happens to be an attorney.

"You should be." He finally takes a long drink of scotch. "If you worked out a deal with an investor or two, your business would be on its way. You need money for marketing and promotions. You can't expect to sew every design yourself forever. You have to start looking at the big picture."

His words don't sting. Tyler and Cadence sat me down a few months ago and gave me the same speech. They want to invest too but I've been wary of mixing business with such a close and important friendship. I consider them my New York family and if I were to lose the money they invest in me, I'd never forgive myself.

"You want to work at this full-time one day, don't you?" He presses on when I don't respond immediately. "If you keep waiting, you might miss your chance to hit it big. Your tomorrow can be today, Sophia. I can help make it happen."

His words are encouraging even though the idea of having his money backing me feels like a recipe for relationship disaster. "It wouldn't be good for us."

"For the dating us?" He cocks his left brow as a smile ghosts his lips. "Our business arrangement would have nothing to do with that."

It's not that cut and dry. I know all about what happened to Evlin Dawn and her husband when they launched Bluenix. Six months later her brand had a spread in Vogue and her husband was in the Caribbean with a model they'd hired for their print campaign.

"I don't think we can separate the two, " I say honestly. "What happens when we break up and you have to come to shareholder meetings?"

His smile fades. "We're adults, Sophia. We can handle it. If we can't I'll send a liaison in my place."

"A liaison?"

He eyes the people seated at the bar. "My sister. Nyx will take over controlling interest of my shares if it ever gets to that point."

I don't know much about his family other than what I found online. There was mention of his sister, Nyx, in one article but I only skimmed it looking for details about the man sitting next to me. "Does she have better fashion sense than you?"

His gaze skims the jeans and blue button down shirt he's wearing. He'd slid out of his wool coat once we sat down. "What's wrong with my fashion sense?"

"Joe won the best dressed contest tonight," I point out wryly. "At least he wore a suit to meet me."

"He was meeting us," he corrects me. "I assume he came here straight from his first day of work at Foster. Besides, I had no idea if we were hanging out here or in a room."

I lower my voice to a purr. "The night is still young, Mr. Wolf. If you play your cards right, I might be able to show you a luxury suite."

He finishes the last swallow of scotch in the bottom of the glass. "You're very resourceful and multi-talented. Speaking of which, tell me you'll think about my offer to invest. We can have Nyx sit in on our business meetings if you want. She's a lot like you. Her entrepreneurial spirit is on overdrive."

I focus my eyes on his. "Does she own her own business?"

"She does," he doesn't elaborate. "You two need to meet. I'll make that happen, but first show me that luxury suite."

Chapter 28

Nicholas

When I asked Sophia to take me up to the room she talked about, I assumed I'd finally get to feel her ruby red stained lips wrapped around my dick. I saw the way she was looking at me in the elevator as we rode up to the top floor. She knew that I wanted her. I made that clear when I hooked my arm around her waist while she stood in front of me in the lobby waiting for the elevator to arrive. When she subtly ground her ample ass into me, my cock instantly hardened.

"What did you think we were going to do up here?" She approaches me from behind, her reflection coming into view in the window's glass. "I noticed you folded your coat over your arm so you could hold it in front of you on the ride up. You were obscenely hard, Nicholas."

I turn to face her. She'd left me alone as soon as we walked into the suite when her phone rang. I thought she'd ignore it in favor of dropping to her knees, but she politely excused herself and took off into another room, closing the door behind her.

I listened, but the walls in this place shielded her voice completely. I didn't think anything of it until a full fifteen minutes dragged by and I'd had my fill of the view of the city from the wall of windows we're standing in front of.

"I'm not anymore." My hand skims over the front of my jeans. "Do you need to put out a fire? That call seemed important."

"It was."

I wait for more of an explanation, but she's quiet as she stares over my shoulder at the darkened view of Central Park.

"So your boss owns this place?" I ask, knowing that talking about sex is only going to irritate the hell out of me. I want to fuck her. I've wanted it since she walked into the hotel and took off her coat. Her body is amazing and since I've been inside of her, I have to work to control the constant need I feel when I'm near her.

Her gaze pulls away from me as she surveys the impeccably decorated suite. "I think he forgets that he does. He's got a lot on the go."

It's hard to imagine anyone forgetting that they own a place like this. I'm not easily impressed, at least not at this stage of my life. I can stay in a suite like this without a second thought to the cost but I rarely do. I don't see the purpose when I'm traveling alone. If I had Sophia by my side, it would be different. I'd want to give her the best of everything, but she'd never let that happen. She manipulated the situation with Joe in order to stay out of my debt. It's clear that she doesn't want to owe anyone anything.

"Do you like working for him?" I ask as I study her profile.

She turns to look at me, her blue eyes locking on mine. "Sure. Gabriel's a good boss."

He must be if he allows her unfettered access to this suite. We didn't stop anywhere on our way up here. She had the key card in her purse the entire time which means she uses it on a regular basis.

"Who else have you brought here, Sophia?"

She keeps her eyes on me although her top lip quivers so slightly that it's virtually unnoticeable. I see it because I can't take my eyes off of her.

"No one," she confesses in a low tone. "I come here myself sometimes."

"Yourself?"

"Mr. Foster's mom stays here when she's in town." She tilts her chin toward an open door that I assume leads to a bedroom. "I'm usually at her beck and call. I do it because Gabriel asks me to but on the day she leaves I always arrange a car service for her. Once I know she's gone, I come here and order the most decadent dinner on the menu and watch the sunset out these windows."

"You bill your dinner to her stay?"

She sucks in a breath before she nods once.

I bark out a laugh. "How fucking amazing is that? I love that you break the rules."

Her eyes stay trained on my face for a few seconds longer before a bright smile slides across her lips. "Gabriel's mom left two hours ago so you and I are splitting a Wagyu beef and Foie gras burger with a side of the best fries cooked in truffle oil you'll ever taste."

***

"You've got it all figured out, haven't you?" I look down at Sophia as we walk toward my apartment. "I saw the way you joked with the guy who brought our food up to the room. He obviously knows you're not Gabriel Foster's mom. You don't seem worried that he'll fuck up your free room service plan."

"He won't." She shakes her head, her hands bunching up the scarf around her neck to pull it tighter. "I'm in charge of Mr. Foster's annual symphony subscription. When he isn't planning on attending with his wife, he hands off the tickets to me. Sometimes I go but if I don't, I give the tickets to other people who work for Mr. Foster, including the man who brought our food."

"You bribe your fellow employees with tickets?"

"You make it sound dirty." Her perfectly arched brows wiggle. "I consider it a fair exchange between friends."

I hold onto her elbow as we cross the street, guiding her around a group of pedestrians crossing in the opposite direction. "What else have you gotten in exchange for those tickets?"

She blinks as she comes to a stop on the sidewalk. "One time when I took a pair of tickets to the manager of the Liore boutique she gave me a bag full of imperfect samples that Mr. Foster had told her to trash. There was absolutely nothing wrong with any of those panties except some snags in the lace."

"You'll have to show me those snags."

Her lips twitch as she tries to suppress another smile. "You already have a pair of my panties. You can check out those."

I do have a pair. I tucked them into the top drawer of my nightstand after she left the other night.

"By the end of tonight, I'll have another pair to add to my collection."

"Is that an invitation?"

"It's a promise," I exhale before I kiss her softly, my tongue parting her lips so I can taste her. "Come home with me, Sophia."

"How can I say no when you kiss me like that?"

Chapter 29

Sophia

I knew even before he closed the door of his apartment behind us, that I'd take Nicholas in my mouth. I'm no expert when it comes to oral sex. I much prefer receiving to giving, but that's because most of the men I've slept with haven't had mouth-watering dicks. Nicholas Wolf is a definite exception. I've thought about licking and sucking his cock since we met and tonight, I'm about to make that happen.

"You haven't said two words since we got here, Sophia. What's on your mind?"

I have been quiet. I sat next to him on his leather couch and listened to him tell me about his next book tour. It sounds both exhilarating and exhausting. I've never been to most of the places he's listed, although I'd love to go to Paris. I've always envisioned myself there, participating in Fashion Week with a show of my own.

"Nothing." I look down at my lap.

"I've told you before that you're a shit liar." He turns toward me. "Something's changed. You look nervous as hell."

"I'm not a liar." I close my eyes to shield the truth from him. "I'm also not nervous."

I can sense movement and then I feel his soft lips press against mine. "We don't have to fuck, Sophia. We can just hang out if you'd prefer."

My eyes flash open to meet his. "I don't prefer that. It's just…"

"It's just what?" he interrupts me with a sigh. "I want you to relax. I want you to have fun when you're with me. Right now you look like you're ready to explode."

My gaze catches on the trio of picture frames on the table near the piano. I want to ask him about the girl in the photograph. I haven't dwelled on the mystery of who she is but it's a thought that has crossed my mind since the last time I was here.

"You look like you're in another world." His index finger brushes my chin. "Does this have to do with that call you took when we were at the hotel?"

It doesn't. The call was personal. I should explain it to him but now isn't the time. I'm not about to ruin our evening with the dull story of the one endlessly annoying issue that keeps popping back into my life. If this thing between us lasts beyond a few weeks, I'll confide in him, but until then I see no reason to. "No. It's not about the call."

"Is it about me?"

I tilt my head to look at him. He's not asking me that because he believes he's the focus of my every waking thought. I see the concern in his expression. If I didn't know better, I'd bet money on the fact that Nicholas Wolf is wondering if I'm about to dump him.

"Why would it be about you?"

A smile ghosts his mouth. "You weren't happy that I hired Joe to help you. I thought maybe you wanted to give me shit about that."

"I handled that like a pro if I do say so myself." I brush my hand across my shoulder. "You get all of your money back and I get a new website for free. We both win in that deal."

"You also got my tech guy a job, so he won't be able to work on my stuff as easily as he used to."

I shoot him a look. "Don't be selfish, Nicholas. Your website makes mine look like a clown show."

"You've seen my website?" He inches closer. "Has the stalked become the stalker?"

I rest my hand on his thigh. "You'd like that, wouldn't you? It would make your day if I chased after you."

"It would make my year." His hand moves to cover mine, sliding it up his leg. "I can't think of anything better in life than being pursued by you."

"I thought I already caught you." I look down at where our hands are now resting on the top of his thigh.

He tugs me closer. "You have. I'm yours to do whatever you want with."

"In that case…" I run my lips over the stubble covering his jaw. "Stand up and drop your pants."

***

He didn't drop his pants in the living room. Instead he took my hand and walked me to his bedroom. I wasn't sure if he missed the inference in my words, but I didn't care when he stripped me naked and went down on me first.

I'd never tell him to stop when his head is perched between my legs. Instead, I propped myself up on my elbows and watched him eat me out. His eyes fluttered open occasionally and the hum of his groans only spurred me closer to the edge.

The man knows what he's doing and he proved that in spades when I came, the sheets of his bed clenched in my fists.

Now, he's on his back, spread eagle in the middle of the twisted sheets with his swollen cock resting against his body.

"This is beautiful," I say quietly as I kneel next to him. "Not all men have cocks that look like this."

"I'll take your word for it." He opens one eye to peer at me. "I haven't seen a lot of them."

I skim my thumb over the purple-tinged crown smearing the large drop of pre-cum that's been tempting me. "I've seen a few."

"Just a few?"

I've never told anyone my number. I don't think that's what he's asking but I'm not ashamed of the fact that I've had only a handful of lovers in my life. "Yes, a few."

He doesn't press for more. His eyes flutter closed as he relaxes his back against the dark linen sheet with his arms crossed over his head. "Suck, Sophia."

The words are direct and heated. It's not a command, although it doesn't border on a request either. It's a plea. I can hear that in his voice. He wants this just as much as I do.

I lean forward and run my lips over his cock before I part them and trace the same path with my tongue.

He gifts me with not only a hot-as-fuck growl but a hand in my hair. He twists the strands between his fingers. "In your mouth."

I do it, slowly. I inch my lips over him until I can't take anymore. His hips rise from the bed as he seeks more so I circle him with both hands and pump. I pump and I suck, my head bobbing up and down as I try to find a rhythm that matches the one of his body.

"I need my fingers inside of you when I come. Give me your pussy," he bites out on a ragged breath.

I do. I inch my knees closer to the edge of the bed, never once letting his cock slide out from between my lips.

I whimper when I sense the light brush of his touch against me. He moves and then I feel the sensation of wetness and warmth. He must have licked his fingers to ready them for my tender flesh.

I pump harder and swirl my tongue around the head of his cock as he slides two fingers inside me. I can't stop my body's need so I rock back and forth, fucking his long elegant fingers as he fucks my mouth, each stroke deeper than the last.

He thrusts harder when he nears his release and the second I feel the crest swell under my tongue, I move away from his touch because I don't want anything to steal this from me. I relax, close my eyes and enjoy every last drop.

Chapter 30

Sophia

I put on the button down shirt he was wearing before he took me to bed. He'd thrown it on the floor on top of his discarded jeans and belt. After he came, I crawled up his body so I could rest my head on his chest. He was spent, laughing softly about how I'd drained him dry and he needed a nap to recharge before he'd make sure I was satisfied.

I don't know a woman who wouldn't be satisfied by his tongue or the taste of him. I've never done that before for a man and now all I want is to do it again.

I quietly pad down the hallway barefoot in search of something to drink. I know that he keeps the glasses in a cupboard over the stove and a pitcher of cold water in the refrigerator. I get both, finishing off the entire glass of cool liquid in one long gulp.

A small green light flashes across the room and it takes me a second to realize that it came from the alarm panel. Nicholas armed it when we arrived, just as he's done every time I've come over.

The building I live in has a doorman but beyond him and the deadbolt lock on my door, I've never feared for my safety. Nicholas has taken extra precautions with this place which I assume is because of all the beautiful artwork that is hung on the walls.

I cross the room to find my purse. I'd left it on the coffee table earlier when we were sitting next to it. I reach in and fish for my phone. I doubt that there's anything that needs my attention now but since my date for the night is passed out cold in the other room, I might as well draft some of the emails I have to send out to Foster executives in the morning.

The light from my phone's screen illuminates the area around me and my eyes instantly gravitate toward the frame. The frame itself may be unremarkable but the picture that it's showcasing isn't. I get up and move to the chair next to that table where the frame is. I turn on my phone's flashlight, shining it directly on the picture of Nicholas and the mystery girl.

I pick it up, hopeful that a closer view will offer more insight into who the dark haired beauty is. It doesn't. I cradle it in my hands, my gaze riveted to the smile on the face of the man who is fast asleep in a bed down the hall. It's the same man who obviously clings to something in his past that this photograph represents.

I fumble with the frame as I'm about to set it back down. I gasp when it falls from my hands. I reach forward, grabbing the corner just before it hits the floor. I breathe a heavy sigh of relief because I don't know how in the hell I would have explained to Nicholas that I dropped the picture and broke the frame all because I couldn't keep my curiosity in check.

I cradle it in my hands, my gaze sweeping over the back of the frame and a small white corner of something peeking out from behind the dark backing board. I tug on it carefully and more of it comes into view. It looks and feels like a piece of paper.

With trembling hands, I curve my fingers around the small tabs that hold the backing board in place. I move each, being careful not to damage them. It's obvious that the frame itself is fragile. It's not expensive. I've seen a row of similar frames for sale in the drugstore for just a few dollars each.

I tuck the fingernail of my index finger under the edge of the backing board to free it. It takes some pressure before it finally moves and a white paper spills out onto my lap.

I stare at it, suddenly unsure if I should be looking at it. This isn't my business. It doesn't matter that I just had sex with Nicholas. This is obviously something that is private to him and I have no right touching it.

"Sophia."

My head snaps up when I hear his sleepy voice call for me. I listen carefully for footsteps but I hear absolutely nothing.

"I was just getting a glass of water, " I call back as I try and shove the paper into the back of the frame, but my hands are shaking so violently that I can't tuck it all back into the small space behind the picture. "I'll be right there."

"I'm coming to find you." His voice is louder.

I stare down at the frame as I attempt to close the backing board but most of the white paper is still visible. I tug it back out, fist it in my hand and put the frame back together right before Nicholas rounds the corner from the hallway.

***

"You're going to cook for me right now?" I duck my hand into my purse and drop the paper in its depths. "It's really late. I should head home."

I don't actually want to go home. I want another chance to put that paper back in the photo frame where I found it. Guilt is eating at me from the inside out. It started as soon as he walked over to the chair I was sitting in and kissed me. It hasn't let up in the five minutes since.

When he motioned for me to stand, I did. I kept my fist closed, hoping he wouldn't ask why. He didn't bother. He only wanted to embrace me. I stood and let him take me in his arms, relaxing in the moment.

"I'm hungry." He pats his firm bare stomach above the waistband of the gray sweatpants he's wearing as he stalks toward the kitchen. "Our dinner was good but it was hours ago. I could go for some pancakes."

I could too but I have to work in a few hours and besides, I need to formulate a plan to get him out of the room long enough that I can cram that paper back into that frame. The only reason I dropped it in my purse was that I could sense how badly my palm was sweating from anxiety. If there's something sentimental written on that paper, I don't want the ink to run because of me.

Turning my head I see him standing next to the stove, a wire whisk at the ready in his hand and a huge grin on his face. I cave because eating pancakes in the middle of the night with a shirtless Nicholas Wolf should be on every woman's bucket list. "I'll stay for pancakes."

"Get over here and help me." He twirls the whisk in his hand. "I sense you're a better cook than I am."

"I'm not," I concede as I close the distance between us. "Cadence tried to teach me how to cook but it was a waste of time. Not everyone is destined to be a great chef."

I watch as he takes a carton of eggs and milk from the refrigerator before grabbing a few dry ingredients from his generously stocked pantry. "You're in charge of mixing, Sophia. Try not to fuck it up."

I laugh when he hands me the whisk. "Don't you have an electric mixer?"

With a serious expression on his face, he reaches over to squeeze my bicep through his shirt. "You've got the muscle power to do this by hand unless you don't think you have it in you to beat a few eggs."

"I have it in me." I flex my arm even though it's hidden under the fabric of his shirt. "Give me those eggs and I'll beat the hell out of them."

I jump when an unexpected loud buzzing noise fills the room.

"What the …"

"Shit. That was the intercom." Nicholas flicks on a light switch that bathes the living room in soft light. "My brother must be here."

"Your brother?" I call after him as he sprints down the hallway, disappearing in his bedroom.

I take a deep breath when I realize how I'm dressed. I can't meet a member of his family dressed in one of his shirt and panties. I start my own trek down the hall almost running right into Nicholas as he exits his bedroom in a hurry. "Where are you going? You're not leaving, Sophia."

He's dressed in a T-shirt now, in addition to the gray sweatpants he was wearing earlier. On his feet are blue sneakers and a ball cap covers his head. "You're dressed. I need to get dressed too."

"No," he murmurs as he kisses my forehead. "I'm going down to the lobby to talk to Sebastian. I'll get rid of him. Then we can get back to making pancakes."

"Sebastian?" I repeat his name. I read a few small details about him online. He's the brother who followed in the footsteps of their father to become a NYPD detective. He's older than Nicholas by two years and judging by the picture I saw of him online, there's a definite family resemblance.

A frown knits his brow. "I haven't told you about my brothers, have you?"

"Not yet. You told me about your sister."

I'm startled by another loud buzz from the intercom.

"He's as impatient as fuck. He sometimes comes by after his shift to shoot the shit. I'll go down to the lobby and tell him to go to hell."

I pat his shoulder, relieved that I'm going to have a few minutes alone to put that piece of paper back in the frame before he realizes it's missing. "I'll wait right here for you."

"You better." He stares at me. "I don't want you to ever leave."

My weak knees almost give out with the words but I stand tall and watch him walk toward the alarm panel. He disarms it with two button punches before he exits out the apartment door without turning back.

I don't waste a second before I'm at the couch, my purse in hand. I fish through it, easily pulling the white paper out. I study the crumpled mess, my eyes focusing on several small red dots that pepper the surface.

I take measured breaths, wanting to calm my racing heart. The debate is strong inside of me. I know I shouldn't open it, but the need to see what it is wins the battle over my better judgment.

I unfold it carefully, each movement revealing more red dots; some small, others larger.

Once I smooth my hands over it on my lap, I read the words written by a feminine hand.

I can't wait to be your wife, Nick. I'll love you until my last breath. Briella. xx

Briella.

A beautiful name for a beautiful woman who loves the man I can't get enough of.

I want to know who she is and why the note she wrote him looks like it's covered in specks of blood.

175

Chapter 31

Nicholas

"Why are you dressed, Sophia?" I stop just inside the door of my apartment and arm the alarm. "I told you I didn't want you sneaking off."

"I waited for you." She slides her coat over the blouse and skirt she's put back on. "It's not exactly sneaking if you wait."

My throat works on a hard swallow. She's different. Something changed between the time I left to talk to my brother and now. It was no more than ten minutes, but Sophia went from being open and willing to be guarded. "Did something happen while I was gone?"

She looks up at me, her eyes haunting. "I looked at the time. I have to be in the office early today because Mr. Foster has a conference call."

"It's hours until daybreak." I press the pad of my thumb against her lower lip. It's pale now. She didn't take the time to apply any lipstick. She looks disheveled and beautiful. All I want is to take her back to my bed. "You can sleep here for a couple of hours and I'll make sure you're back at your place in time to go to work."

Panic flashes across her expression as she steps back. "I need to prepare for that call. It's not as simple as dialing him into it. I have files I need to pull. Gabriel likes everything to be in its place when he arrives in the morning."

It's bullshit. Something spooked her while I was gone. "What did you see, Sophia? Did you find something?"

"Nothing," she spits out too quick, too eagerly.

I trace a path around the room with my gaze trying to find something that could have caused her to retreat like this. "You saw something while I was gone. I want you to tell me what it was."

With a muted curse, she shakes her head. "Are there things in here I shouldn't see?"

Other than my next manuscript, there's nothing that I'd want to shield from her. I keep everything I treasure in my office. I have items stored there that I haven't looked at in years. Those are the things I have no intention of ever showing anyone. "I can't think of anything."

Her eyes give her away. They dance between my face and the area near the piano. I turn to look in that direction. "What is it? Is it something over there?"

"It's nothing." She tries to take a step around me, but I move to block her.

"I don't play games." I look down and into her pale blue eyes. "You're running because something freaked you out. I want you to tell me what that is."

"I said it's nothing," she hisses between clenched teeth.

I pull her closer to me. "It's written all over your face. Spit it out. What the fuck happened after I went to the lobby?"

"Nicholas," she says my name, exasperation marking her tone. "Have you ever been in love?"

I don't have to turn back to the piano to know what she saw. It's the picture of Briella and I. Anyone looking at that picture could see what we shared. "Yes, I loved a woman once."

"That woman?" Her hand flies in the air past my head. "Is that the woman you love?"

I don't take comfort in the obvious pain in her tone. I know Sophia's falling for me. She's on the brink but I've already taken the leap. I'm crazy about her, every single part of her including this jealous streak I see now. "I loved her once. It was a very long time ago."

"You don't love her now?"

It's a simple question with an answer that is complex and complicated. I open my mouth to respond but the words aren't there. I've never said aloud that I don't love Briella. I haven't considered whether I still do or not. "It's not easy to explain, Sophia."

"It is easy. Do you still love Briella?"

Irritation mixes with anger inside of me. I try to level my voice but it's fucking useless. There's no way she would know Briella's name unless she pried that frame apart.

"Fuck," I mutter under my breath as I turn and stalk toward the table. I hear Sophia's heels clicking on the hardwood behind me.

"Nicholas," she says my name quietly. "I…I was just so…"

I scoop the frame into my hand and turn it over. The normally visible corner of the paper isn't in view. She opened it. She read it. She put her hands on the one thing I haven't touched since that day.

"You opened this." I wave the frame in the air in front of her face. "Did you open this? Did you fucking read the note, Sophia?"

Her gaze follows the path of the frame. "I saw there was something in the frame. I wanted to see what it was."

"You had no right." My heart races, my vision blurring. No one on this earth knows I have that note. They can't know. "What the hell were you thinking touching something so personal?"

Her bottom lip quivers but she stills it with a bite from her top teeth. "I was curious. It's the only picture you have on display that isn't of your family."

She's right. I don't have dozens of photographs of friends. There isn't one picture from any of my book signings in my place. I like things simple and for me that includes reminders of the people who matter the most to me; my siblings, my mother and Briella.

"You didn't think to ask?" I clutch the frame to my chest. "Why didn't you just ask me who she is? Why touch things that don't belong to you?"

She shifts, inching more to the side. "I think I should go."

I reach forward to grab her arm to halt her in place, but she sidesteps me. "You're not leaving. You need to answer my question."

"I didn't think you'd tell me the truth."

"I'm not a liar."

"I didn't say you were." She tilts her head and studies my face. "I asked you earlier if you love her still, and you didn't answer. You're not a liar, Nicholas. You're an avoider."

It's nothing but a stall tactic. She wants to get out of here without telling me why the hell she thought it was okay to take this frame apart. "Why did you read the note? Answer me, Sophia."

A single tear falls onto her cheek. "I don't want you to break my heart."

Fuck. Fuck this beautiful woman.

I toss the frame onto the chair and pull her into my chest. I cradle the back of her head as I feather kisses over her cheeks. "I'm not going to break your heart. I want in it, Sophia. I want in your heart and I want you in mine."

"What about her?" I watch her index finger rise in the air as she points at the frame. "What about Briella?"

I close my eyes and swallow back the rush of emotions that flood me. "Briella died, Sophia. Her father killed her."

Chapter 32

Sophia

Death isn't something I've had a lot of experience with. I still have every single one of my grandparents, I've never lost a friend and because of my mom's severe allergies to pet dander, we never got to have a dog or a cat when I was growing up.

For me, death is restricted to the hour of television I watch with Cadence each week where someone is murdered and our favorite duo of police detectives crack the case with time to spare for the prosecution to present its case and get a conviction.

I stare up and into the face of the man I know I'm falling in love with. I knew it before I took that frame apart and saw the love letter written to him by another woman. I knew it earlier tonight when we were sharing a dinner and laughing about how great it would be if I started the next fashion trend.

"I don't talk about her anymore." His hands cup my cheeks as he speaks softly. "She died when I was in college. It's been a long time."

A long time is subjective when a heart is involved. He couldn't tell me if he loves her still because a part of him does. I can see that in his face but I see something else there too and all of that is directed at me.

"Her father killed her?" I ask because I'm still trying to process that. My dad cherishes me. He might not be happy about the fact that I'm living on my own in New York City, but I know he'd do anything in his power to protect me.

He caresses my upper arms through my coat. "He shot Briella's entire family. There was only one survivor. Her sister pulled through."

"Is he in jail? Did her dad go to prison?"

Letting out a deep breath he looks down at the frame before he responds. "The bastard shot himself last. Thankfully he didn't survive."

It's a tragedy of epic proportions. I want more details. I want to understand how he found out and why the note Briella wrote to him is covered in a spray of something that looks like blood. I bite my tongue though because now isn't the time to ask about details that don't matter anymore. He lost someone he loved in a horribly violent way.

"Can we go back to bed, Nicholas? I just want us to hold each other until I have to leave."

He nods his head slowly. "I want that. I want you, Sophia."

***

"You're talking about the Vanderwelle family, Soph." Cadence butters a slice of toast. "I remember when that happened. It was a couple of weeks before Christmas. The entire Northeast was in mourning over that."

I wouldn't know. I was living in Florida eight years ago when it happened. I didn't pay any attention to the news. I don't know a lot of sixteen-year-old kids that do. Apparently, Cadence is one of them.

"Our school had a fundraiser." She chews on a small bite of her omelet. "One of the daughters survived and a woman who lived near the family set up a collection for her hospital bills and recovery. We sold pins in the shape of small hearts. We raised a lot of money for her."

Life intersects in the most unexpected of ways sometimes. "I can't imagine what that girl went through."

"I met her last year." She takes a sip from the glass of milk she ordered. "She came into Nova with her husband. I recognized her from the pictures in the paper and then when she introduced herself, I knew it was her. Lilly Parker is her name."

"Lilly Parker?" I ask, after sampling the scrambled eggs I ordered. I'd texted Cadence to meet me here for my brunch break. After I hopped in a taxi after kissing Nicholas goodbye I went straight to work. I changed into the dress I keep in my locker there and after a quick brush of my hair, I was sitting at my desk, ready to get to work when Mr. Foster came in at seven.

It's near ten now and since the conference call went off without a hitch, I asked if I could take lunch early. He agreed and even offered me an extra hour since he was in such a good mood.

"That's what I said." Cadence hits the bottom of the mustard bottle on the table, aiming it at her toast.

"Are you going to put mustard on your toast?" I scrunch my nose.

"Firi likes that," she says it without breaking a smile. "He has unusual taste."

I shake off the thought of what that tastes like and instead circle back to Lilly. "I worked with Lilly when I was at Hughes Enterprises."

I'm instantly struck with the image of the petite redhead who runs the tech department at the company I worked for when I first came to New York. We didn't interact very often because I was an assistant to one of the other executives, but she was friendly and helpful. I had no idea that she'd lived through such a personal hell.

"I don't know her beyond a few words when she came to Nova, but she seems grounded. I don't know how I'd survive losing my entire family in one night. I don't think anyone can ever get over that."

I don't either. It's a horrific experience like that would be branded into someone's memory forever. Both Lilly and Nicholas lost people they loved that night. That has to create a bond that is as unbreakable as it is unique.

Chapter 33

Nicholas

"You look much better with the glasses, Nicholas. You should always wear them," my mother says as I sit next to her on the patterned sofa she bought when I was a kid.

I've offered to fix up my parents' place, but they've always told me that there's nothing wrong with the apartment they live in. They're right. It keeps them warm in the winter and the noisy air conditioner my father installs in their bedroom window keeps part of the place cool in the summer.

Aesthetically, it's a trip back to a time twenty years ago. The entire place needs a facelift, but I've learned through the years, that the décor is a moot point only in my eyes.

"I met someone."

I don't look in her direction when I say it. My mom has standards for her sons that none of us will ever meet. It's likely the reason the three of us are all still single.

"A woman?"

The question is ridiculous. It's also a buffer between her surprise and the response that is sitting on the tip of her tongue. I've only ever told my mother about two women in my past. Briella was one and the other was a fleeting infatuation that lasted no more than a day after I confessed my feelings for her to my mother.

She shifts in her seat, clearing her throat in the most vocal way possible before she spits out the three words I know are coming. "It's a crush."

"I'm too old for a crush," I toss back with a wide smile. It's the smile she craves when I walk in the door. She knows I want her approval in every aspect of my life, including the women I date. That's why I rarely mention them. There's no need to open that door unless I'm prepared to step through it by introducing her to the woman in question. "This is more. I'm crazy about her."

She nudges her own glasses back up the bridge of her nose before her hand sweeps over her brown curls. "What's this girl's name?"

"Sophia," I go on, "Sophia Reese. She's beautiful and talented."

"Aren't they all?" she asks barely under her breath. "What does Sophia Reese do?"

She makes me want things I thought I'd never want again. She makes me feel like there's hope.

"She's an executive assistant at a company downtown." I purposefully avoid specifics so I can focus on the future that I know Sophia is carving out for herself. "She's also a fashion designer."

"A designer?" My mom's eyes light up. They're the same blue as mine, but hers are surrounded by the fine lines that come with time and worry. "What does she design?"

"Clothing for women." I dig my phone out of the front pocket of my jeans. "I'll show you her website."

I type in the address to Sophia's site and I'm greeted by a new design. Joe's obviously paying off the debt he owes. The site looks cleaner and the navigation is simple and precise.

"You can see some of her designs here." I hand the phone to my mother. "She's going places."

Her gaze drops to the screen of my phone, her finger busily scrolling through the dress, skirt and blouse designs. "Your girlfriend does good work, Nicholas. When are you going to bring her around?"

It takes me a beat to answer. "Soon. I'll talk to her about the four of having dinner."

"I'll cook the dinner." She pats the top of my hand. "No need to spend money for no reason. I'll make my pot roast and your girl can tell me all about the world of high fashion."

***

"You didn't think this was something worth mentioning before?" Sophia darts up onto her tiptoes and kisses me. "I can't believe this, Nicholas."

I can't believe this gorgeous woman just kissed me in the middle of the street. I grab her elbow and hurry her to the curb before we both get run over by a delivery truck headed straight for us.

"I wasn't sure if you'd be receptive." I adjust the scarf around her neck. "You got riled up when I asked Joe to help you."

"Joe is Joe." Her eyes shine with excitement. "Claudia Stefano is not Joe."

She's right. Claudia Stefano just happens to be one of the most influential women in the fashion industry today. She's also a fan and when I crossed paths with her earlier today after I left my folks' place, I mentioned Sophia to her. She was receptive to the idea of meeting with her as long as I agreed to be there.

Claudia and I have struck up a friendship of sorts. It's not close. We rarely see each other, but there's a familiarity between us that works. I send her copies of my new books and she raves about them on social media. Considering her own following numbers in the tens of millions, a good word from her is guaranteed sales.

"We'll have dinner with her next Wednesday."

"I should wear something special." Her eyes scan her heavy wool coat. "I might have to work on something new. This is Claudia Stefano, Nicholas. Claudia Stefano."

"You could wear anything you've already designed and she'd be impressed." I brush my fingers against her cheek. "You're going to blow her away."

"You know she just opened a new string of boutiques, right?" She bounces up and down on her heels. The nervous energy flowing through her is palpable. "I read in Vogue that she's on the hunt for new designers to showcase."

"I could come over to your place to see your designs." I haven't pushed her to let me see more of her world. I know that when we first met she was wary of how close I got to her, but things have changed. We have changed.

"You could." Her lips purse. "I could make you some pancakes."

"Tonight?" I push because I want that access. I want to be invited into her life in a way I haven't been before.

"I can't tonight." She sighs. "I didn't realize I'd see you today."

I surprised her on her way back to the office at lunch. I was heading there when I spotted her outside a restaurant talking on her phone. As I approached, her smile widened and the call ended. "We'll do it another night. I have another surprise for you. We can talk about it the next time I see you."

"We'll talk about it now." She grabs the lapels of my jacket in her fists. "What's the surprise?"

"My mother wants to meet you."

All of the color drains from her face instantly. "Your mom?"

I know it's early for that, but I'm not against breaking dating code with this woman. "I told her about you earlier. She loves your designs."

"You showed her my designs?"

"I showed her your new website," I make a point of mentioning that. "She loved the designs and the site. Joe did a good job."

She nods, but her mind is somewhere else. She's contemplating, considering. "Do you think she'd like me? I mean beyond my clothing designs, do you think your mom would like me?"

"I know she will," I fire back quickly. "It doesn't have to be an event. She wants to make dinner, but I can easily convince her to meet us for brunch on the weekend or lunch one day if you want a guaranteed escape. I think I'll invite my sister too. It would be good for you two to meet since I still want to talk about investing in your business."

"We could all meet at a place close to the office." Her voice is serious. "If we did it in a couple of weeks, would that be okay? I need to focus most of my time on the new dress I'm going to design for our dinner with Claudia."

    I smile to hide the disappointment. I'm moving this too fast. She's feeling pressured. I see it in the way her shoulders have tightened and her hands have fisted in front of her. "We'll do it whenever you're ready, Sophia. No rush. Take all the time you need."

Chapter 34

Sophia

"You're full of it, Sophia." Dexie Walsh finishes the last sip of wine in her glass. "You're just saying that you're going to have dinner with Claudia Stefano because of that picture of Libby Duncan holding my purse at her latest movie premiere that went viral online. You're totally trying to one up me."

"First off," I begin as I wiggle my right index finger in the air. "That picture didn't go viral. It barely got a thousand views on that fashion blog, Dex. Secondly, I am having dinner with Claudia Stefano and it may benefit you too and lastly, I loved that purse Libby Duncan was holding. It was one of your best to date."

She pushes her hip against my kitchen counter. "Let's pretend you are actually having dinner with Claudia Stefano. Explain how that would benefit me."

I roll up the towel in my hand and toss it in her direction. "Dry the plates."

"Let them drip dry." She places the towel on the counter next to me. "We could have eaten out of the take-out boxes. You didn't have to set the table."

I reach for the towel and give each of the two plates I just washed, a quick dry before I place them back in the cupboard. "We have dinner once a month. It's always the same take-out. I wanted this to be a mini celebration in honor of my impending meeting with Claudia."

"It's Claudia now?" she quips. "You two are on a first name basis already?"

"Nicholas calls her that. They're friends."

I study Dexie's face as she considers that. Her blonde hair is streaked with pale pink. The color does little to accent her dark eyes, but they still pop. Dexie works full-time in the marketing department of Matiz. We met through Crew initially, but as soon as we realized that we both have a love of fashion, our connection took on a life of its own. Dexie designs handbags and crafts them all in a small studio uptown. She's offered me a corner to work on my own stuff, but the space is too cramped and I'm much more comfortable here, in my apartment with my sewing machine and over a thousand square feet all to myself.

"I still can't believe you're fucking Nicholas Wolf."

I feign a sigh. "We do more than fuck. We date."

"You eat dinner and then you fuck, right? Isn't that what dating is?"

I turn toward the living room. "Technically, I guess that's a big part of it, but he wants more already. Today he told me that his mom wants to meet me."

"Already?" She pours more wine in her glass. "You two just met."

It's been a few weeks, but she's right on point. It's early in our relationship and meeting a parent is something I've only done once before. In my world, that's reserved for something more serious than a few dates and a handful of moments of intimacy.

"I like him a lot," I confess. "He's told me some stuff about his past that helped us get closer. I think he sees the same potential with me that I see with him."

"What stuff did he tell you?" She tucks her hair behind her ear. "Is it juicy? Should I pull up a seat?"

I wave toward the living room. "Be my guest, but I'm not sharing. He told me things in confidence and I'm not breaking his trust."

"Some friend you are." She giggles. "Forget him then. Tell me about Claudia."

I laugh at her use of the designer's first name. "Nicholas is taking me to meet her for dinner next Wednesday. I'm going to design a new dress and I thought if you wanted, I could use one of your bags as an accessory."

She reaches forward to hug me. "You're not fucking serious, are you? Tell me this is real."

I push back on her shoulders and gaze down at the pink, long sleeved off the shoulder shirt she's wearing. I designed it for her months ago and virtually every time I see her now she's wearing it. Tonight it's paired with worn blue jeans. Often, she'll be wearing it with a black skirt. Besides Cadence, Dexie is the only person who is as excited about my designs as I am. "This is as real as it gets. I need something tasteful that will go with the new black dress I'm designing."

"I have a clutch that I think you'll love. I can drop it by Foster tomorrow on my lunch break."

"This dinner could change our lives forever, Dex."

"If it does, you'll need to thank Nicholas for both of us." She wiggles her perfectly arched brows.

***

"Are you here for the piano or me?"

I smile up at him. He's been sleeping. I can tell by the way his hair looks and the fact that he's wearing nothing but a pair of black silk pajamas. I came over to his place right after Dexie left my apartment. We'd worked side-by-side for two hours on a sketch of the new dress I want to wear when I meet Claudia.

Dexie had contributed with the random nod of her head or wince. By the time we were done, I had a design that I know will impress the woman Nicholas has arranged for me to meet. If this design doesn't get my pieces a spot on the rack in one of her boutiques, I don't know what will.

"I'm here to show you my latest design." I look past him to his darkened apartment. "Can I come in?"

"If you promise to strip as soon as I close the door, the answer is yes."

I laugh as I push past him. "I wanted to show you this so badly. I should have called first to see if you were awake."

"I settled in early because I'm getting up at dawn to finish the rough draft on my next book."

"*Action's Cause?*"

He huffs out a laugh. "I finished that one up seven months ago. The one I'm working on now is the follow-up to that."

"What's it called?" I ask excitedly even though I've yet to read more than the first chapter of *Burden's Proof*.

"That's between me and my publisher."

I smile when he winks at me. "You don't have a title for it yet, do you?"

"Fuck, no. I'm stumped. Throw out some ideas for me."

"For a title for your book?" I eye him suspiciously. "You know that I have absolutely no talent when it comes to stuff like that."

"That's what makes you perfect." He leans forward to kiss me softly. "You don't have any skin in the game. You're impartial."

"In that case, I need to read some of it to get a better idea of what I'm working with."

He wraps his fingers around my wrist, his touch soft and gentle. "You're not serious, are you?"

I know how much it would mean to him for me to show more of an interest in his work. He's gone out of his way twice to help me with mine. He set me up with Joe and a week from now I'll be breaking bread with one of my fashion idols and it's all because of him.

"I want to read it."

"Now?"

I didn't expect that. I assumed we'd make love and then I'd show him my sketch but he needs this more than I need his approval on a dress that I already know is spectacular. "Now."

"Wait." His thumb runs across my cheek. "I'll take you to bed first, make you come and then you'll tell me whether you think my next book is a fucked up mess or not."

"That's a deal I can't possibly refuse."

Chapter 35

Nicholas

I fist her ponytail in my hand as I take her from behind. I've been inside of her before but it's never been like this. I'm deep. I'm so deep that with every drive of my cock into her tight wet pussy, she cries out my name.

"You like it this way," I whisper in her ear as I fold my body over hers.

She only moans in response so I up the tempo, driving my dick into her in long, easy strokes. This woman was made to be fucked. Her body is sensual and ripe; her ass enough to send my heart racing. I skim my palm across one cheek before I grab the lush flesh in my fist.

She moves back trying to take more from me.

I haul her up and into me, grabbing her left tit from behind. I squeeze it, the nipple furling into a tight point beneath my fingertips.

"Oh, God." She reaches down to circle her clit with her finger but I want to see her face.

I turn her over quickly before I sink back into her. "I want to see you come."

She opens her eyes as I fuck her. Her gaze locked to mine. She's the most beautiful thing I've ever seen. Her lips parted slightly, her hair stuck to the side of her face and her eyes lost in the moment of pure pleasure.

I pump harder, wanting her to come before I do.

She lets out a low moan and just as I feel her pussy clench around me, I lose it, coming inside the woman I'm now sure I'm falling in love with.

***

"This is better than *Burden's Proof*." She turns away from my laptop screen to where I'm lying next to her on the bed. She's sitting cross legged in just a pair of panties with my computer balancing on her thighs. If this isn't what a writer's wet dream is, I sure as fuck don't know what is.

"You actually like this one?" I ask suspiciously. "Are you just saying that because we fucked earlier?"

Her ass squirms on the sheet. "I'm still sore from that."

I don't apologize. There's no fucking way I will. I was deep inside of her. I loved every minute of it. She did too. "I'll kiss it better later."

"Promise?"

"I don't have to promise to eat your pussy, Sophia. I'd do it all day if I could."

"How would you write?"

I huff out a laugh. "Good point."

She nods as her gaze drops back to the screen. "I have a question about the book."

"Ask away." I rest one of my elbows on the bed to raise my body.

She hesitates before she turns to look at my face. "Did you model the character of Julia after me?"

I didn't. I wrote Julia's character weeks before I met Sophia. I wrote her to honor Briella. I have a character in every book that I silently use to pay tribute to the first girl I ever loved. Julia is fierce and untamed. She's a young woman driven by her passion to succeed. She's everything Briella was. "I actually wrote the parts with Julia before we met."

"That makes sense." She laughs off my response. "She's so vivid. I just thought that she must be written about someone so I assumed..."

She stops herself as her gaze falls back to the laptop's screen. "This is so good, Nicholas. I'd like to read the entire thing."

"Be my guest."

She puts her hand on my cheek. "It's almost morning. I have to go to work in two hours. As much as I'd like to spend all day in bed with you reading this masterpiece, I can't."

I glance back at the clock on my bedside table. I must have been lying next to her for hours as she read. "I'll give you one to go."

"To go?" She giggles as she watches my nude body as I jump to my feet.

"I'll get a flash drive and save you a copy." I round the bed to where she is. "Don't move. I'll be right back and as soon as I have the book saved for you, I'm going to say good morning to you the right way."

"What's the right way?"

I look down at my now erect cock. "What do you think?"

Chapter 36

Sophia

"What if she hates the dress?" I stare at my reflection in the full length mirror in the hallway of my apartment. "I wish I would have chosen a different belt to go with this."

Cadence glances down at the screen of her phone. "You have time to find another belt. You're not supposed to meet Nicholas and Claudia for another hour yet."

I take a step back and turn to the left. "I don't know, Den. What do you think about the one I'm wearing?"

She walks up behind me and rests her hands on my shoulders. "I've already told you twice how much I love the dress. The belt is just an accessory, Soph. It's the dress that's going to impress Claudia."

I know she's right. I've worked on the dress non-stop for over a week now. I sewed every black pearl onto the bodice by hand and I painstakingly took my time with the scalloped neckline. This is, by far, the most beautiful piece I've ever created and I'm hopeful that once Claudia Stefano sees it, we'll be having a conversation about a trial run of my line in her stores.

"Have you heard from Nicholas yet?"

I turn around to look directly at my best friend. "The last time I spoke to him was two days ago. He was finishing up the draft on his latest book.

He told me he'd be in the zone so I shouldn't expect to hear much from him until tonight."

"He's intense, isn't he?"

He is. It's one of the things I love about him, or think I love about him. I've been trying to convince myself that the depth of my feelings aren't real but our time together this past week has been sparse and I've missed him more than I've ever missed anyone before.

I've been busy working on my dress and he's been engrossed in his writing. It's been hard since most of our contact has been sporadic text messages. I did promise him I'd spend the night with him tonight after we're done having dinner with Claudia. It's been the prize at the end of the finish line for me. I can't wait to feel his arms around me.

"You're daydreaming about him again." Cadence laughs. "You're in another world right now, Soph."

"I'm nervous," I confess on a sigh. "This is the most important night of my life. I get one chance to impress Claudia. If this goes well, I can launch my career tonight."

"You're going to launch your career tonight," she subtly corrects me as she adjusts the silver pendant I'm wearing. "This is a once in a lifetime opportunity and you're nailing it. You have the dress, you have the man of your dreams by your side and you're going to walk out of that restaurant with a deal in place to show your designs at the boutiques of one of the most influential women in the world."

Before I told Cadence last week that I was having dinner with Claudia, she had no idea who the woman is. The fact that she's done her research this week to understand the magnitude of this meeting has not only impressed me, it's touched me deeply. She's now as invested as I am in the outcome of tonight.

"You should have a glass of wine before you head out."

I glance up at her face. She's so calm. She's been my voice of reason since she rented me a room in this apartment more than two years ago. She knows exactly what I need. "I'll have two sips of wine to calm my nerves and then I'll go show Claudia Stefano why I'm the next big thing in fashion."

"That's my girl." Cadence hugs me tightly. "Before this day is over, your entire life is going to change."

***

"I believe the reservation is under Wolf," I say to the woman behind the small podium that sits just inside the doors of Hibiscus, a new restaurant that just opened on the Upper East Side.

She scans the computer screen in front of her. "I don't see that name here."

"It must be Stefano then. I'm meeting Claudia Stefano for dinner."

She doesn't bat an eyelash which isn't surprising. The little black dress she's wearing is obviously straight off the rack of a major department store. It's unremarkable in every way.

"I'm sorry, but there's no reservation in that name either."

I fish for my phone in the small gold clutch that Dexie loaned me for tonight. "The only other name you can try is mine. That's Reese."

She nods slowly. "Let me try that one. Our system is new. Something might have gotten mixed up when the reservation was made."

I don't look at her as my fingers race over the screen of my phone. I pull up my contact's list and scroll down to his name. I dial Nicholas with a push of a button.

"Again, let me apologize." The woman behind the desk tosses me a sympathetic look. "Perhaps you can call the people you're meeting?"

Apparently, the fact that my phone is next to my head isn't a clue that I'm doing exactly that. I take a step back from the podium and listen to ring after unanswered ring.

"Nicholas, it's me," I whisper when his voicemail finally picks up. "I'm at Hibiscus and something's happened with the reservation. Call me as soon as you get this."

"Miss?" The woman behind the podium calls out to me as I drop my phone back into the clutch. "You're more than welcome to take a walk around the restaurant to see if your party is here. As I said, our reservation system has had a glitch or two since opening and I'd hate for you to miss your dinner because of that."

I follow her in silence as she leads me into the packed dining room. I survey the faces of each patron, quickly looking them over in a desperate attempt to find Nicholas or Claudia.

"I don't see them." I turn back to the hostess. "Is there another dining room?"

"We have two private dining rooms." She waves her hand to the left. "There's a shortcut through the kitchen. Follow me."

I do. I fall in step behind her as she weaves her way around servers before we take a straight path through the crowded kitchen.

We walk down a short corridor before I hear the raucous voices of a group of people who are all gathered in an alcove around a large dining table.

"I take it those aren't your friends?" The hostess tosses me a smile.

I shake my head. My voice is stuck somewhere between my stomach and my throat. If Nicholas and Claudia aren't in the other private room, I have no idea what I'm going to do.

An earpiece the woman is wearing buzzes suddenly, causing her to stop in her tracks. "I have to take this. All hell broke loose back at reception. The other dining room is straight ahead and to the left."

I stand in place as she walks away.

There's no sound drifting from the dining room to my left. I smooth my hands over the skirt of my dress before I take a step forward and then another. Just as I turn to look into the dining room, I stop moving.

The only person standing there is Nicholas. He's facing me. His hands are tucked in the front pockets of his jeans. His face is impassive.

"Nicholas?" I rush toward him. "Where's Claudia? I was so scared I was going to miss this."

He raises both of his hands in the air as I near him. "Stop. Don't fucking touch me."

I freeze in place, my heart racing. "Nicholas?"

"I told Claudia who you really are, Sophia. She wants nothing to do with you."

My stomach knots. "What does that mean? What's going on?"

"You play innocent better than anyone I've ever met." He chuckles. "I fell for it. Fuck, did I fall for it."

"You fell for what?" Anger simmers inside of me. "I want to know what's going on."

"What's going on is your career is over. I spoke to Gabriel an hour ago and if you haven't heard yet, you're fired. Claudia is going to make sure that your designs never see the light of day in this town."

My knees go weak. This can't be real. How is this happening? I look down at the dress I'm wearing. This is the dress that was supposed to launch my career. "Mr. Foster wouldn't fire me. He wouldn't do that to me."

"It's done. You're done, Sophia."

I search his face trying to understand what the fuck he's talking about. "You're not making any sense, Nicholas."

"I'm not making sense?" He clears his throat. "You stole from me. You took that manuscript I gave you and you sold it and now you're going to pay the price for that."

"What manuscript?" I search his face for reason but all that's there is bitter rage.

"You're not getting out of this by playing the naïve card."

"I'm not playing any card," I scream at him. "You're scaring me. I don't know what you're talking about. I swear, Nicholas."

"Let me make it crystal clear for you." He steps toward me, his hands bunched in fists. "Two people had access to that book I let you read while you were naked in my fucking bed. Those two people are you and me."

I nod. "I remember reading it."

"Do you remember fucking sell it to the highest bidder?" His voice is edged with sarcasm.

"Sell it? Why would I sell it?" I haven't touched the flash drive he gave me since I put it in my purse at his place. I've been too focused on creating the perfect dress for tonight.

"I don't know why you sold it." He brushes past me. "All I know is that the book made its debut on a streaming site this morning and my lawyer will see you in court."

"Court?" I twist around and grab his elbow to stop him." What does that mean?"

"You know what it means." He tugs his arm free. "I knew I couldn't trust you. You never once invited me to your apartment. That was the first red flag."

"I was nervous," I confess. "That's a big step for me."

"It's a fucking excuse. I knew the second I realized you put your hands on the note Briella wrote that this wouldn't end well for me. I should have listened to my gut. I wish to hell I would have."

I don't say a word. I stand in stunned silence as the man I love turns and walks away taking every single one of my dreams with him.

THANK YOU

Thank you for purchasing my book. I can't even begin to put to words what it means to me. If you enjoyed it, please remember to write a review for it. Let me know your thoughts! I want to keep my readers happy.

For more information on new series and standalones, please visit my website, www.deborahbladon.com. There are book trailers and other goodies to check out.

If you want to chat with me personally, please LIKE my page on Facebook. I love connecting with all of my readers because without you, none of this would be possible.
www.facebook.com/authordeborahbladon

Thank you, for everything.

ABOUT THE AUTHOR

Deborah Bladon has never read a romance hero she didn't like. Her love for romance novels began when she was old enough to board the bus, library card in hand to check out the newest Harlequin paperbacks. She's a Canadian by heart, and by passport, but you can often spot her in New York City sipping a latte and looking for inspiration for her next story. Manhattan is definitely her second home.

She cherishes her family and believes that each day is a gift for writing, for reading, and for loving.

Made in the USA
Middletown, DE
27 July 2017